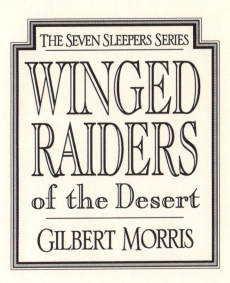

THE SEVEN SLEEPERS SERIES

WINGED RAIDERS
of the Desert

GILBERT MORRIS

MOODY PRESS

CHICAGO

To Daisy and Rocky—
two swell cats!

Contents

1

A Plea for Help

L ook out, Sarah—you're going to lose him!"

Sarah Collingwood had been dozing, holding her fishing pole lightly in her hand. At Josh's yell she made a wild grab for the pole. It slid across the grassy bank and hit the water with a splash. Sarah cried out, "Oh no—!" staring at it.

Josh Adams, age fifteen, was a tall, gangly boy. He had auburn hair and dark blue eyes—and loved to fish. With another yell he plunged into the water, stabbed at the swiftly disappearing pole, and managed to catch the end of it. "I've got it!" he yelled excitedly. "I've got it!"

Sarah watched Josh splash back to the bank, slipping in the mud once and falling headlong. He struggled to his feet, rolled over to a sitting position, then hauled up sharply on the pole. It bent double, and he held it with both hands yelling, "Sarah, it's a real pole-bender!"

Sarah danced around crying out advice as Josh held onto the pole. Finally, with a mighty heave Josh sent a wet fish right into Sarah's face. It knocked her over backward, and she grunted, "Umph!" Falling headfirst, she tried to brush the fish away, but it seemed determined to nestle inside her clothing. "Get him off of me, Josh!" she screamed, shoving desperately with both hands. Josh stood up, muddy from head to foot, and began to laugh. "Hang on to him, Sarah. I think he likes you. He must think you're his momma."

Sarah finally managed to push the fish away and stood up, her eyes flashing. She was a small girl of fifteen, the same age as Josh. She was very graceful, but her brown eyes flashed with anger. "You did that on purpose! Look—it's got my hair all slimy." She pulled her hand through her long black hair and patted it. "I ought to throw that fish back."

"Not on your life!" Josh picked up the fish carefully and took it off the hook. It flopped mightily, and the sun caught its silver scales so that they flashed and made a beautiful sight. Holding it up, Josh said, "Look, isn't it a nice one? I think that will feed you and me, and we already have enough for all the others."

Sarah was still peeved and walked over to the clear stream that trickled over mossy rocks. Kneeling down she washed her hands carefully and then dabbed at her face. "Well, I'm not going to clean these fish," she declared. "You'll have to do that."

"No way," Josh said. "We made a bet, remember?" He pulled a stringer up, added the fish to it, held it up, and admired the fish, flopping and trying madly to escape. "The one that caught the most fish doesn't have to do any of the cleaning," he said. "I've caught six, and you've caught three. That means you lose."

Sarah gave him a disgusted look, then shrugged. Suddenly a light came into her eyes, and she smiled slightly. Stepping a little closer to him she put her hand on his arm and said softly, "Joshua, I just thought of something."

Josh stared at her suspiciously. "When you talk soft like that," he said, "I know you're going to try to get me to do something—but you won't."

"Oh, Josh, you know how I hate cleaning those nasty old fish! If you'll clean them for me, I'll make you a fresh pie tonight—all your own."

Josh's face lightened. "Well now, that's business," he said. "But it has to be apple, though, with cinnamon, just like I like."

"That's a deal," Sarah said quickly. She smiled and patted his arm fondly. "Come on, let's go home. It's getting late anyway."

They followed the path that traced its way along the stream. They talked about the fishing trip, and when they came in sight of the house, Josh said, "You know, I wouldn't care if we stayed here for another month. I'm tired of going out on quests and fighting dragons and things like that."

Sarah giggled and looked at him mischievously. "I don't remember you fighting any dragons," she teased. "That was Reb, if you'll remember."

Josh reached over and hit her lightly with his fist. "Never mind that. Living in the caves of Mondar was enough adventure for me," he declared. "Remember those T-rexes?" He gave a shiver. "They had teeth six inches long, just like sharpened knives. They could bite a horse in two."

Sarah nodded. "I wonder how they're getting along? They were good people, weren't they, Josh? You usually think about cave people as being thickheaded—but they're not. They didn't know as much about some things as we did. Down deep, though, they were just like us."

The two walked along thinking of the adventure they had just had. They were part of a group called the Seven Sleepers. The group had been miraculously preserved, surviving a nuclear war. They had awakened in a world they had never imagined, filled with strange beings, and discovered that they had slept for many, many years. All things were changed now. Earth was gone, and the place they now inhabited was called Nuworld.

They discovered that they had been preserved to serve a strange man called Goél, a leader who fought against the powers of darkness that threatened to overcome the world. Many adventures they had known, facing

9

danger and trial, often failing but learning to trust in the power of Goél. They had just returned from a strange land inhabited by primitive people. They had been glad to get back to a very nice house. Goél said before he left, "You need rest. Enjoy yourselves. Someday I will come again, and you must once again go forth to combat the powers of darkness."

Now as the two young people moved along, light-hearted and laughing, they were suddenly alarmed by a horseman that burst out of the dense woods to their left. He was upon them almost before they knew it, and Josh saw that he was a fierce, warlike man.

"Look out, Sarah!" he yelled, for the stranger had drawn a shining sword that flashed in the red rays of the dying sun. Josh threw himself in front of Sarah, wishing desperately that he were armed. Now there was nothing he could do but try to stand between the warrior and Sarah. "What do you want?" he cried out, standing straight.

The warrior was mounted on a fine, clean-limbed horse that looked swift as the wind. He was not a large man but slender and muscular. His eyes were almost black, and he swept the two with a careful glance. His skin was darker than usual, burned golden by the sun. He had a black beard and trim mustache. He wore a light robe that was almost white and reminded Josh at once of pictures of inhabitants of the desert back in Oldworld.

"What is your name?" the rider demanded.

Josh ignored the whirling sword that was held almost at his chest. He was afraid but was determined not to let it show. "My name is Adams—Joshua Adams," he said. "Why do you come at us with a sword? Are you a bandit?"

For one moment the lean, tanned bronze face of the rider relaxed, and his white teeth showed as he smiled. "No, I'm not a bandit. If I were I would have what I wanted from you already."

Sarah stepped from behind Josh. "What is it you want?" she demanded.

The rider examined the girl carefully and seemed to like what he saw. "You have courage," he said. He nodded as if pleased and added, "I like that." He sat on his horse for one moment, then seemed to make a decision.

In one swift move he came off the animal in a smooth, gliding motion. He slipped his blade back into the sheath at his side, then shoved the hood back from his face. His hair was black as hair can be, and he was a handsome man, though somewhat the worse for wear. He looked tired, and when he spoke again his voice sounded weary. "My name is Abdul," he said. "I serve Chief Ali Shareef."

"Ali Shareef?" Josh shook his head. "I've never heard of him. What's he the chief of?"

"My people live far away," Abdul said. "As you see, my steed is weary." He slapped the coal black stallion fondly on the shoulder and said proudly, "It takes a long, hard ride to tire him out."

"Who are you looking for?" Sarah asked. She had appeared frightened at the rough appearance of the heavily armed rider, but now she came to stand beside Josh saying, "If we can help you, we will."

Abdul stared at her. "I seek Goél," he said and watched their faces. "Do you know of such a one?"

Sarah and Josh exchanged glances, then Josh nodded. "We are the servants of Goél."

"Good!" Abdul seemed to sigh with relief. He suddenly seemed very tired, and his lips grew white. He leaned against his horse, and his head drooped. "I-I want to—" He grabbed at the horse and seemed to be falling.

Josh leaned forward and held him up. "He passed out—or he's about to!" he cried. "We've got to get him back to camp."

"Let's see if we can get him back on his horse—then we can lead him in." Sarah came up and asked, "Can you hear me, Abdul?"

He didn't answer but nodded slightly.

"Come on, Josh, help me boost him up."

The two youngsters managed to get the warrior back in the saddle.

"You lead the horse, Sarah. I'll get on behind him and hold him." Josh leaped up behind Abdul and supported him so that he would not fall. "All right, let's go."

Ten minutes later they reached the small rest house, set back in a grove of trees. As Sarah led the black steed into the yard, the house seemed to erupt with young people. The first out was Bob Lee Jackson, age fourteen. Bob, whose nickname was Reb, was a tall young man with pale, bleached hair and very light blue eyes. He wore a white cowboy hat and came at once to help Josh get the man out of the saddle.

When he spoke, his voice had a distinct Southern twang. "Well, where in the cat-hair did you come up with this one?" he demanded. He was very strong, and between the two they helped the man to a chair on the porch. "He looks like he's done run out of spizerintum—and he sure does look thirsty."

A small-boned girl of fourteen, Abigail Roberts, ran at once to get water. She was a pretty girl with light blue eyes and fine blonde hair, very conscious of her appearance. She brought a glass of water and put it to the lips of the stranger.

He drank thirstily, and when he opened his eyes she smiled at him. "There—is that better?"

Abdul swallowed, then looked around. "Yes, much better." He looked at Josh and said, "Are these your friends?"

"Yes, that's Bob Lee Jackson with the funny hat, and this is Abigail Roberts. This little guy here is Wash." He indicated a small black boy no more than thirteen who had come to watch with round eyes. "And this is Jake Garfield."

Jake was small—the same age as Abigail and not much larger. He had flaming red hair and alert brown eyes.

"And my name is Dave Cooper." The speaker was the largest and obviously the oldest of the young people. At sixteen, he was tall, athletic, and handsome enough to have been a movie star back in Oldworld. He had yellow hair and blue eyes and looked down curiously at the visitor. "Where did you spring from?"

Josh interrupted. "His name is Abdul and he's looking for Goél. He's come a long way, he says."

Jake demanded, "What do you want with Goél?" He was a suspicious boy by nature, and some of the hard adventures he had undergone had made him more so. He looked around, and his eyes narrowed. "How do you know he's not a spy?"

"Oh, Jake, you'd be suspicious of your own grandmother!" Wash said in disgust. "Give the poor fellow a chance, can't you?" He was almost diminutive, certainly not as long as his name, which was Gregory Randolph Washington Jones. There was a kindly light in his light brown eyes. "Don't pay any attention to Jake." He smiled, his white teeth flashing. "He was born suspicious."

Josh had been the leader of the Sleepers from the beginning, except for those times when Goél had indicated otherwise. Now he said, "You're obviously tired and haven't eaten. Suppose we fix you something and afterward you can tell us about yourself?"

"That would be good," Abdul said. "I am very hungry. I've not eaten in two days."

13

Josh said, "Well, I've got enough fish for all of us. Come on, Jake, you and I'll clean them. The others can get the rest of the meal thrown together."

The Sleepers at once became very active. They were all curious about the visitor, and Abbey insisted on leading him inside and putting him in an easy chair. She sat down and talked with him while the meal was being prepared. Finally she came and whispered to Sarah, "Isn't he the handsomest thing! He looks like a desert sheikh."

"Yes, he's nice looking all right," Sarah said, putting a platter of fried fish on the table. "I wonder what he wants with Goél?"

At that moment Josh came in and said, "Looks like supper's ready. Come on, let's get at it. Abdul, you sit right here. I hope you like fried fish."

Abdul sat, his eyes going over the food, and soon he and the others were eating heartily. Josh kept the conversation going, but every eye kept going back to the man of the desert.

Finally Sarah brought out two pies and said, "Josh, you'll have to share your pie with everyone else."

Josh's face fell, but he shrugged. "All right, I guess I'll have to do it then. Sure hate to give up my pie though." He ate his slice, and when he had finished he leaned back and said, "Well, Abdul, if you want to tell us your story, I guess we're ready to listen."

Abdul's face was relaxed. He had been listening to the talk of these young people and seemed somehow to understand that he had nothing to fear. "I come from far away," he said. "My people are being enslaved and killed by the Winged Raiders."

"The Winged Raiders! Who are they?" Jake demanded.

"They are the raiders of the desert," Abdul said, his lips growing tight.

"Why are they called the Winged Raiders?" Wash asked.

Abdul seemed surprised. "Why? Because they have wings!" he said. "Why else would one call them that?"

"You mean, like real wings? Like birds?" Reb asked. "Yikes, that'd be something!" His blue eyes gleamed, and he shook his head. "To be able to fly like a bird—I've always wanted to do that!"

"I wish these could not fly," Abdul said slowly, "but they can."

"You called them raiders." Josh said. "Exactly what do they do?"

The Sleepers sat quietly as Abdul told how the strange beings came sweeping out of the sky, raiding his people. "They steal our young people and take them away, and we never see them again." His face fell, and he said, "My own brother was taken away when he was very young." Angrily he slapped the table. "They take our crops, they take our people—we live in fear. They must be stopped."

"Why did you come to us?" Josh asked. "Is it that you seek help from Goél?"

"There is a song that some of our people have heard," Abdul said slowly. "It says that one day the Seven Sleepers will break the power of the dark ones. We have heard this, but no one understands. I alone asked our chief to let me come." He looked around the circle and said, "You are the Seven Sleepers?"

"Yes, we are," Josh said quickly.

"Then you must come. Otherwise we will perish."

"We can't go unless Goél commands us," Dave said at once. He shook his head, adding, "We're under his command."

Abdul began to beg, "Surely he wouldn't say no. Can you not ask him? We understand he is a good force and that wherever he goes, peace follows."

"He comes and goes when he chooses," Sarah said. "We have no way of calling him."

Abdul seemed to slump in his chair, his face grew weary, and he shook his head. "You are my last hope. If you will not come, I think our people must all perish." He looked around and said, "I must go back to them."

"Wait!" Josh said quickly. "You're tired and your horse is tired. Rest a few days. Perhaps Goél will come. If he does and if he commands us, we will come and help you."

Abdul nodded slowly. "That would be good indeed. I will hope that Goél will come—and that he will send the Sleepers to help rid my people of the raiders of the desert!"

2

Without Authority

"Jake," Reb said in disgust, "you're as stubborn as a blue-nosed mule!" He was spinning his lariat expertly and suddenly launched it out so that it fell over Abigail, who was walking by.

She squealed, and Reb laughed. "Gotcha that time!"

Abigail stared at him with disgust, removed the rope, then walked away with her nose in the air.

"I'm not stubborn," Jake stated flatly. "I'm just careful—that's all." He was putting together a machine that he vowed would catch fish automatically. Reb and Josh had both said they'd rather pull them in on a line. Jake, however, loved to invent things. He slowly pulled a lever, but it snapped, catching his finger. "Ow!" he yelled, hopping around first on one foot, then on the other.

Reb laughed. "Well, it might not catch fish, Jake, but it sure caught you. Here, let me get that little hummer off of your finger."

Jake stopped long enough to allow Reb to disengage the apparatus and then stuck his finger in his mouth. He glared down at the invention, reached over with his free hand, and picked it up. He heaved it as far as he could, then shook his head. "That would have worked if I just had the right kind of stuff to work with." Removing his finger from his mouth, he looked at it. "Wouldn't be surprised but what it was broken." He grunted and looked over to where Abdul was sitting on a rock about thirty feet in front of the house. "How do we know he's who he says he is?"

"How do we know he's not?" Reb asked, pulling his rope in. He began to spin it, making a fancy S-shape and then threw it up in the air. It seemed like a live thing in his hand. "Why would he lie about a thing like that?"

"He might be a spy of the Sanhedrin," Jake grumbled. "You know how terrible that Elmas is. He'd do anything to lead us into a trap. He's almost done it two or three times."

"I don't think Abdul is a spy."

"You never think anybody's a spy. You're too trusting. That's what's the matter with you, Reb. Remember that sorceress that nearly got you chewed up by a dragon? Didn't you learn anything from that?"

Reb flushed, for he had been deceived by what appeared to be a fair young woman back when they were visiting a land called Camelot. "Well shucks! You don't think Abdul's a sorcerer, do you? Haven't you listened to anything he's said?"

"Yes, I have," Jake said, "and I don't say he's wrong, and I don't say he's a spy. All I say is we can't go running off every time somebody walks in and asks us to come and save them."

The argument had been going on for three days. Most of the other Sleepers had gained confidence in the visitor. They found Abdul to be an honest man, strong and obviously very courageous. He had come on a long and dangerous mission for a very noble purpose. Jake, however, had stubbornly refused to agree. And now he shook his head and added, "We'd be crazy to leave here on some wild goose chase. And that's what I'm going to say when we take a vote."

Reb looked up in surprise. "You reckon we're going to take a vote on this?" he inquired. "I thought Josh would just make the decision by himself."

"He says he can't do it. It's too much responsibility."

18

"Well, I reckon it is. When are we going to vote?"

"I think we ought to vote right away, and I think we ought to vote no."

The vote came quicker than either of the boys expected. When they ran back to the house, Josh stepped out and said, "Everybody gather around. I've got something to say."

He waited until they came close, and he looked at their faces. "I guess you pretty well have your minds made up about Abdul here." He looked over at the stranger, who had stood to his feet. "Abdul, if you don't mind, we have a little private business—"

"Of course," Abdul said at once. "I will go for a walk. Call me when you make up your minds."

Josh waited until Abdul was out of hearing distance, then said quickly, "We've got to do something. Abdul's going back to his people in the morning, and we've got to decide whether we're going with him and try to help."

Immediately Jake said, "Wait! We can't go without the command of Goél. We all know that."

Wash answered, "You don't know that Goél wouldn't want us to go. He's just not here to say. I think we ought to go with him."

Josh looked around the circle and said, "Well, personally I do too, but I can't make the decision alone. We're going to take a vote. Everybody in favor of going with Abdul to the desert, raise your hand."

Immediately every hand was raised—except Jake's. He glared around and shook his head stubbornly. "I vote no," he said. He stood there scowling at the others almost angrily. "I thought you all had more sense! Say he's all right. Maybe he is, but that doesn't matter. Every other quest we've gone on, we went because Goél told us to go. And now you want to go out and do it on our own. I think that's a pretty good way to get us all killed."

"Wait a minute!" Dave said quickly. "You're right, Jake, that Goél has always *told* us when to go, but we know where he stands. And these Winged Raiders sound like they're connected with the Dark Lord to me, and you know Goél's against him."

"That's right," Sarah added quickly. "At least we can make a start and go talk to the chief. Goél has a way of showing up when we need him."

"That's what I say," Reb Jackson said quickly. He was a young man who liked action and was getting bored. "I think we can handle these Winged Raiders." He nodded confidently. "I mean, after all, back in Oldworld I used to go out hunting quail. I didn't have any trouble with them."

Josh shook his head cautiously. "I think these are a little more dangerous than quail," he said slowly. He looked around the circle, his eyes coming to rest on Jake. Biting his lip, he said, "Jake, it takes nerve to stand alone, and I recognize that. But the rest of us all seem to be agreed. Since helping these people seems like something Goél would *want* us to do, I think we've got to go and expect that he will meet us somehow either on the way or after we get there." He gave Jake a curious glance. "You don't have to go, Jake. You could wait here if you want."

Jake threw up his hands in disgust. "I'm the only one with any sense!" he declared. "I'll go, but I won't like it, and that's all there is to it." He turned and walked away, his back straight with anger.

Josh stared after him. "We won't make up our minds now. This is a big decision. Maybe Goél still will come before Abdul leaves in the morning. I sure do hope so!"

Wash said, "I'll go get Abdul, but can I tell him we'll go with him?"

"No, I'm just not sure," Josh said. "We won't decide till morning."

"All right."

Wash ran down the road and found Abdul standing beside the creek, looking down it. Abdul turned to face the young black boy. "What did you decide?" he asked at once.

Wash was embarrassed. He said, "Aw, well—most of us want to go, but—"

"But some do not," Abdul said. "How will you decide?"

"Well, Josh—he's kind of the leader," Wash said. "He wants to go, but he's just afraid to go without an order from Goél directly. He's our leader, you see."

Abdul nodded. "It is good to follow your leader." He seemed heavy and disappointed and began to walk slowly back to the house.

"Tell me more about your people," Wash said, "and about these Winged Raiders. What do they do?"

Wash listened carefully as Abdul spoke of the grief and pain—and even death—the Winged Raiders of the desert had brought to his people. He spoke of families being robbed of their children, of some being killed. Those who had been captured never returned except once in a great while. Only twice, he said, there had been escapes. They had told horrible tales of brutality, torture, and slaves being worked until they died and then thrown carelessly aside.

Wash listened for a long time, and finally when Abdul stopped he said, "You know, my people were slaves a long time ago."

"They were?"

"Yes, there was a great war fought, and finally my people were all set free to be like other men." The small boy's face twisted, and he shook his head. "I don't like to think about anybody being a slave." He looked at the tall man. "I know Goél would want us to go set your people free." He saw that Abdul still looked discouraged and said quickly, "Don't worry—it will be all right. You'll see! In the morning we'll be going with you."

They returned to the house, and no one said much to Abdul that night. They saw that he was despondent, and Josh whispered to Dave, "I see he thinks we're not going, but I think we have to. What do you think?"

Dave shrugged. "I'm like you, Josh. We know where Goél would stand on this matter of kidnapping and slavery. It's a chance to strike out at the Dark Lord. I think we ought to go."

The next morning at the breakfast table Josh said suddenly, "Abdul, we have decided we're going with you."

At once Abdul straightened his back, and relief washed across his face. He looked over at the small dark face of Wash and smiled. "Now," he said, "hopefully my people can be free—as yours were."

* * *

They took a day to get ready to go. Josh insisted they take as much equipment as they could carry. Nuworld had not developed guns and bombs. The weapons here were swords and longbows and daggers. Reb insisted on taking his rope, of course, and early the next morning they mounted their sturdy horses, and Abdul led them out.

"It will be a hard trip," he warned. "We have perhaps just enough provisions to get us there if we're careful."

They traveled hard the first day, stopping at noon for a brief break, and that night they camped beside a river. They ate the meat that they had brought with them and slept hard, for the journey had been difficult. They rose the next morning stiff from the unusual exercise and rode for the next four days as fast as their animals would take them.

Finally, on the fifth day, Abdul drew up and said, "Look! There is the desert. In a few days we will reach my home."

Reb looked out over the vast expanse of sand. "Jehoshaphat! I never saw so much country in all my life. Look at it!"

"Can we get across that, Abdul?" Josh asked doubtfully. "I've heard about people dying of thirst in the desert."

"That is true. It is dangerous, but I know the oases and water holes. You must trust me," he said firmly. "I will get you to my people—and then we must trust you."

They traveled for several days over the desert. Abdul had told the truth. He led them unerringly to watering holes. He found water sometimes by digging in the dry beds of streams. Their provisions grew slim, and only when Abdul killed a wild deer were they able to fill their stomachs again.

And the wind! The deeper they penetrated the desert, the harder it blew. The Sleepers clung to their horses, and their clothing was nearly ripped from their bodies.

"Good place to fly gliders." Dave grunted. "But it makes for hard travel."

"The Winged Raiders use these winds," Abdul called out over the wind. "It carries them from their home, the Citadel, all over the desert."

Finally late one afternoon, when their lips were chapped and dry and the girls could hardly sit on their horses and the boys too for that matter, Abdul cried out, "Look! There is the home of my people."

Josh followed his gesture and saw a group of black tents on the far horizon. "Is that where Chief Ali will be?" he asked through his parched lips.

"Yes." Abdul nodded eagerly. "Tonight you will be honored guests under the protection of Chief Ali Shareef."

"Wouldn't be a minute too soon for me." Reb groaned. He eased himself into the saddle. "I've been riding all my life, but this is the longest ride I've ever made. I'm about ready for some cornbread and pork chops."

Abdul smiled at him. "We won't have that, but I'm sure we'll have nice fresh goat."

Reb said to Abigail, who had just made a face, "Just what you wanted, isn't it? Nice fresh goat. Come on, Abbey—I'll give you the best part of the goat!"

3
The Enemy Strikes

Chief Ali Shareef was an impressive man, tall and stern of face. He wore a white robe, as did most of the men that gathered in the council to greet the Seven Sleepers. The Sleepers themselves were curious about their host. They had been introduced by Abdul and were aware that some of the desert people were suspicious.

"I'm not sure we're all that welcome here," Sarah whispered to Josh. She was sitting beside him in front of a group of elders and wondering what would come next.

"I guess all they have to do is look at Jake," Josh answered almost grimly, "and see that some of us are a little suspicious too. The chief is getting up. I guess he's made up his mind about us."

Chief Ali rose to his feet and focused his dark eyes on the young people. "We welcome you to our home," he said in a deep voice. "My servant Abdul has told us that you have come to help." A frown swept across his dusky face, and he shook his head in despair. "Indeed," he said sadly, "we are in desperate need."

One of the elders, a short muscular man with a bristling beard, spoke up. "Indeed, Chief Ali, we are in need of friends. But I fail to see how these—these children can be of any help."

Another elder spoke. "I agree. What we need is a host of mighty armed men. Only by force will we be able to combat the Winged Raiders."

A murmur of approval swept over the elders, and Josh felt a moment of despair. He waited until the men had spoken, then rose to his feet. "May I speak, Chief Ali?" he asked. When the chief nodded, he said, "We have a saying in our world, 'The race is not always to the swift.' I realize that we seem to be useless to you, but Goél sometimes uses the weakest to overcome the strongest. We have seen him do mighty things when all looked impossible. All we ask is that you let us remain with you for a time."

"You're welcome and will be our guests," Ali said. A smile tugged at the corners of his thin lips, and he added, "We had hoped that Goél himself would come to our aid."

Jake piped up, "That's what I say! And until he comes, I don't believe we can do business."

"Will you shut up?" Reb Jackson whispered, digging his elbow into Jake's side. "We've got problems enough without you making it harder."

Chief Ali, however, seemed amused by the stocky Jake's truculence. "My young friend, you are outspoken. That is not always good, but at least we know where you stand." He swept the Sleepers with his eye saying, "Be our guests. We will learn from you, and perhaps you will learn from us."

* * *

For the next few days the Sleepers had what amounted to a vacation. Reb, more than anyone else, had a blast! The desert people were horsemen, and their horses were strong and swift. They were amazed to find that the young man who wore the outlandish hat was as good a rider as many among their own people. And they were amused at the use of his lariat.

The first morning Reb had demonstrated his skill by dropping a noose over the head of a half-broken pony.

Abdul gasped with surprise. "We have never seen such!"

A murmur of approval went up, and Reb found himself giving lariat lessons each morning and became very popular.

The girls also found themselves the object of much attention. Abigail, with her blonde hair and blue eyes, worked her usual havoc among the young men. They could not take their eyes off her. Abbey, of course, loved the attention and spent most of her time doing her hair in different ways and experimenting with new kinds of makeup. The young girls of the tribe practically fawned over her as she instructed them in the art of beauty.

"I think it's disgusting!" Sarah exclaimed, slumping down beside Josh. "All she does is primp! Can't you say something to her, Josh?"

"What would I say?" Josh demanded. "She's a girl, isn't she? All girls act like that—primping and putting on makeup and worrying about this dress or that."

"Well!" Sarah gasped. "I'm glad to learn what you really think about me, Josh Adams!" She flounced away, and Josh stared after her.

Dave, who had been sitting across from him, said, "Just an old charmer—that's all you are, Josh. You ought to write a book on how to be a Prince Charming."

"Will you shut up, Dave?" Josh snapped. "I don't know what to do with them."

One thing that fascinated the Sleepers was the camels. They were all given riding lessons by Adbul, but none of them did very well. Reb decided that you had to treat camels firmly, just as you treat a horse, and when he went up to his first camel he gave the bridle a jerk.

The camel turned calmly around, looked at him out of soulful eyes, and then spit what looked like tobacco juice right into Reb's face.

Abigail laughed in sudden amusement, and the others could not help themselves. The sight of the vile liquid running down Reb's face amused them all. He'd always been so capable, and now this.

Reb gasped and wiped the mess from his face. He took his hat off and stared at it. He looked around at his friends, who were laughing, and for a moment they thought he would plow into them.

But he had a sense of humor. "Give me your handkerchief, Sarah," he said. Drying his face, he looked at his white Stetson. "At least I didn't get none of that camel spit on my hat!"

They enjoyed the food after a fashion. Mostly it was some form of mutton. The desert people kept large flocks of sheep and herds of goats. One item at every meal was goat's milk, and Wash, for one, couldn't stand the stuff. "What I wouldn't give for a good ol' Dr. Pepper!" he moaned.

"You won't find none of those in this place," Reb said. "I've got to admit, they know how to do a good thing with this here sheep. Although I'd sure like to have a good hamburger!"

On the third day, Josh had a council with the Seven. "I think we've got to do something," he said. They were all sitting inside one of the large black tents on rich and luxurious rugs that covered the sand. They were really comfortable, and it was a great deal like camping out every night.

"What do you mean, Josh—'do something?'" Sarah inquired.

"I've been waiting for Goél to appear and give us some kind of directions—"

"That's what I say!" Jake broke in. "And until he does, we better not try anything."

"I don't agree with that," Dave Cooper broke in. He was lounged back, tall, athletic, and handsome, but now he came to a sitting position. "We've got to do something! Why, we might stay here for a year!"

"That's right," Wash said. "Now that we're here, I say let's do something." He looked at Josh and asked, "What?"

Josh was irritated. "How should I know, Wash? All I know is that we've got to do something."

Sarah said, "I know one thing we need to do and that's to see if we're really fitted for long travel. If we do have to make any long trips, I'm not sure how we'd take it."

Josh smiled at her. "That's right, Sarah. I'll tell you what—I'll ask Abdul if we can make a trek. Just to see how we'd do in the desert."

"Well, I hope we go on horses instead of camels," Reb complained. "I can't get a handle on those hairy critters!"

But Reb didn't get his wish.

Abdul agreed at once to lead the Sleepers on a "maneuver," as Josh called it, and the next morning they started out early. All morning long they bucked the heavy winds that whipped across the desert. They never quite got used to those winds, which blew constantly—sometimes softly, sometimes enough to almost tear away their clothes, but always blowing.

They traveled all day and then reached a pleasant oasis with palm trees and bubbling springs.

That night around the campfire Abdul entertained them with stories about his people. They had a long and honorable history. But finally he shook his head, saying, "We were a great people until the Winged Raiders came. Since then we've been like no more than frightened sheep."

"Where do they come from? Who *are* they?" Sarah asked.

Abdul picked up a stick and began to draw in the sand at his feet. "No one knows. They appeared when I was a boy, and they've been growing stronger ever since."

"I'd like to see one of them critters," Reb said. "Can't imagine a man being able to fly. They must not be men at all," he said. "I think they must be a cross between a bird and an ape of some kind."

They went to sleep rolled in their blankets and the next morning went across the desert again. The sand dunes rolled, white sand almost blinded them at times, and the wind blew. It was about ten o'clock in the morning when Abdul suddenly drew his camel to a halt. "Look there!" he cried out.

Josh, who was right behind him, pulled his camel to one side. They were in a part of the desert that formed a deep depression. At the bottom of it lay a camp by a stream. Tents dotted the sand, and Abdul said, "That is one of the neighboring tribes. They are friendly. Come, and we will let you meet them."

He started down the slope, slipping and sliding, for it was very steep. Bob Lee held on to his camel, leaning back as he would on a bronc.

But Abigail was nearly shaken off and was whimpering with fear by the time they had reached the bottom. "I want off of this thing!" she cried out.

"It'll be all right," Wash said. "Just hang on, Abbey. We'll be—" he broke off and suddenly looked up. "What's that?"

The Sleepers, caught by his voice, looked up, and Abdul gasped. "It's the Winged Raiders!" he said. "They're attacking the camp!"

Josh squinted against the brightness of the sun. They were about two hundred yards from the camp, and he could see overhead what seemed to be nothing more than black dots. As he watched, however, the dots became larger, looking like monstrous birds. "What are they?" he whispered to Abdul. "What are they doing?"

Abdul's voice was subdued. "They are attacking the camp—see, the men are coming out to do battle."

The Sleepers watched as some of the desert people came out armed with swords. A few had bows and arrows. All were looking up, and even from where they stood, the Sleepers could here the cries of wives and children—high piercing cries of fear.

And then Josh got his first look at the Winged Raiders they'd heard so much about. They were far enough away so that they did not attract the Raiders' attention, yet close enough to see. Josh stared in shock as one of them suddenly plunged out of the sky. It was a strange sight that made him gasp. What he saw was a strong muscular form, a coppery-skinned young man with a fierce face. In one hand he held a bow. Across his chest were twin straps that crossed. At his side hung a quiver of arrows.

But the most amazing thing was the huge wings that spread out seemingly fifteen feet. They were like the wings of a gigantic hawk or eagle! They did not beat the air but seemed to catch the breeze. Josh watched the Winged Raider shift his body slightly, which caused him to swerve in the wind. He understood then that these winged ones were gliding rather than flying.

Sarah gasped as the fierce flying warrior loosed an arrow. It pierced the chest of one of the desert people, who fell to the ground and lay still. Other Winged Raiders were dropping out of the sky, loosing their arrows.

"They don't have a chance!" Reb yelled. "We've got to go help them!"

Abdul reached out and grabbed the young man with a steely grasp. "We can do nothing," he said. "They would kill us, just as they are killing my brothers!"

The Sleepers stood there, helplessly watching, and soon it was over. Many of the men lay dead. The Winged Raiders had swooped to the ground and picked up some of

31

the children and young people, then caught the breeze and soared back into the sky like huge birds. They mounted the rising wind currents, and Josh watched, his throat tight, until they became mere dots again, then disappeared.

"Where are they going?" he whispered.

Abdul pointed to a line of mountains that ringed the desert. They rose high in the air, though they were far away. "They are going there," he said quietly. "To the Citadel. That is where they come from."

"The Citadel?" Josh stared at the mountains. "They're nothing but a bunch of murderers! Something's got to be done!"

Jake looked down at the bodies with feathered shafts sticking from their backs and chests. "Well, it's going to take more than us to do it," he said. "Let's get out of here before we get butchered like that! Next time maybe you'll listen to me. We've got to wait for Goél."

Josh shook his head but did not answer. He was thinking, though, as they turned and rode away from the camp. *Maybe Jake's right! Maybe we have jumped out of the frying pan into the fire.*

4
Captured

The shock of seeing the Raiders attack and kill helpless tribesmen was enough to drive Josh into depression. For two days after they witnessed the terrible scene he said little to anyone. Sarah understood. She had known Josh for what seemed like forever. Even back in Oldworld they had been good friends. They had been together ever since they had come from their sleep capsule into the alien Nuworld.

"Josh, you've got to stop worrying about this," Sarah said to him finally. He was sitting out away from the campfire, staring into the twilight as the sun went down. Sarah sat down beside him and put her hand on his arm. "I know you pretty well. You're very upset."

Josh looked at her. In the fading light she looked very pretty, and he thought of how glad he'd been to find that she was one of the Sleepers, when he had first come to this place. He trusted her and was glad that he had a friend who could sense his moods.

"I'm worried," he said. He picked up a handful of sand, held it up, and let it filter through his hand into the other, then tossed it to the ground and brushed his hand against his shirt. "Maybe Jake's right," he said quietly. "Maybe we ought to just leave."

Sarah sat quietly beside him as he talked, and when he fell silent, she said, "I'm just as uncertain as you are. I think we all are. It's one thing to have Goél appear and say, 'Do this,' but it's another thing to go without any specific direction at all."

"I can't understand it." Josh frowned. "He's never left us alone this long. I just don't want to do the wrong thing."

They talked for a long time, and finally Sarah said, "Josh, I can't tell you what to do, but I know I'd rather fail by trying to do something than give up. Nothing's worse than just quitting, is there?"

Josh looked at her and managed to smile. "A baseball player once said don't go down with a bat on your shoulder." He straightened his back, and his mouth grew suddenly firm. "Well, that settles it. We may strike out, but we're going to go down swinging. Come on, let's go talk to the others—and you put a gag in Jake's mouth, would you? He's going to scream like blazes when I tell him what I want to do."

Josh discovered he was right. As soon as he called the group together and said, "I have a plan," Jake began to mutter. Josh overrode him by saying loudly, "I think we're going to have to go to the Citadel."

Then Jake's voice reached a screech. "To the Citadel?" he almost screamed. "Have you lost your mind, Josh Adams? That's where those terrible Raiders are, don't you know that?"

"Of course I know that," Josh said. "That's why we have to go there."

"Why that's like—like—putting your head in a lion's mouth!" Jake sputtered.

Dave Cooper, however, came to Josh's aid. "You know, I've been thinking about the same thing, Josh," he said. "Obviously we're not going to be able to help these people in a physical way. Why, it would take a machine gun to do anything against the Winged Raiders. If we are going to help Chief Ali and his people, it will have to be some other way."

"I think you're right, Dave," Sarah agreed. "It's going

to have to be a matter of the spirit, not of swords or bows and arrows."

The argument went on for a long time, and at first it seemed that Jake would win. He swayed Reb and Wash. And Abigail, of course, didn't want to go anywhere.

Finally, however, Reb came over to Josh's way of thinking. "Why, shucks," he said. "I guess we can't sit around these tents and ride camels the rest of our lives. If you want to go, Josh, I'm with you."

Instantly Wash, who admired Reb greatly, said, "If you'll go, I'll go too!" Finally, everyone except Jake and Abbey agreed.

"You two will have to make your own decision," Josh said. "If you want to stay here, that's fine."

The next morning they met with Chief Ali. He listened, his face expressionless at first, then he broke out exclaiming, "Go to the Citadel? Why, it would be suicide!"

"Just what I've been trying to tell them." Jake nodded.

"I know it sounds like that, Chief Ali," Josh said quickly. "But we found out that sometimes the spirit is more powerful than the sword. We can't be of help to you as warriors. There has to be another way."

Chief Ali's face reflected admiration. He clearly had not expected this and said so. But then he asked, "What will you do? You'll surely be captured and be made into slaves of the Raiders."

"We never know what lies ahead, not even for a day," Josh said thoughtfully. He looked around the group. "You remember how many times everything looked so dark and then somehow we came out of it? Goél's never misled us—oh, I know, Jake, Goél's not here, but somehow I feel that even though he's not with us, this is something he would have us do."

Chief Ali still tried to dissuade them, but they'd made up their minds.

At dawn the next morning, they mounted the camels the chief had set apart, loaded with provisions. "It's a long journey," he said. "I have made a map showing the water holes, but it will still be difficult for you."

"Goél won't let us go astray," Josh said with more firmness than he felt. "Come, we'd better get going." He mounted the camel and hung on while it swayed to its feet. When the others were ready, he looked down and said, "Chief Ali, we will do our best to help your people."

Chief Ali said, "May safety be with you, and may you achieve by the spirit what my people have not achieved by the sword."

The little procession moved out. Soon the camp of the Desert People fell behind the dunes, and the Sleepers saw nothing ahead for miles but rolling hills of sand. Far off, the Citadel lifted its head into the sky. And even looking at it, Josh felt a moment of disquiet.

* * *

"My mouth's plumb dry," Reb said. "Can't even work up a spit."

They had traveled five days and the previous day had found no water. They'd consumed all of their store, which they carried in leather bags, and now all of them were suffering from thirst.

Josh looked overhead where the blue sky looked hard enough to strike a match on. The sun beat down white rays that struck almost like a blow. If it hadn't been for the wind, which had grown steadily stronger, they would have been cooked. "I think we'll find this oasis on the map before dark," he said, trying to look hopeful.

Jake stared at him. His lips were cracked, and his skin was sunburned. "We'd better," he said grimly. "We can't take another day of this."

Josh urged the company on, and all afternoon they

made their way across the shifting sands. The wind blew the sand against their faces, seeming to scrape their skin off at times, and their thirst grew worse. Something like fear began to creep into all of them.

Josh studied the map, but it was hopeless. If there were only some landmarks—trees, mountains, something, he thought in despair, but there was nothing except the Citadel, looming closer as they moved onward. It was still miles away, and even if they got there, Josh knew that there was no telling what danger might come then.

Late in the afternoon when the heat was beginning to grow less torrid, Josh was plodding along, his eyes on the Citadel ahead. It was a towering mountain, like a pile of rocks that seemed to go up to the sky. The sides were sheer. He thought, *Even if we get there, how will we climb up to the top?* He was numbed by the heat and by thirst and fatigue. Looking backward he saw that some of the Sleepers were nearly unconscious, hanging on with the last of their strength.

He turned to look at the Citadel, and as he did, Dave cried out, "Look out—Raiders—up there!"

Josh at once twisted around, and what he saw made his blood run cold. The sky seemed to be filled with winged men. They were so close he could see the glittering eyes. They'd come silently, floating on the winds, and it was too late to do anything about it.

"They're going to kill us!" Abbey screamed.

At once Josh said, "Get off the camels!"

They all slid to the ground.

"Hold your hands up like this!" Josh called. He held his hands over his head and cried out, "We come in peace!"

Some of the winged men had notched their arrows and taken aim, but at Josh's cry the largest Raider called out, "Hold!" in a powerful voice. He shifted his body and made a wide circle, circling the group of Sleepers. His

37

eyes were cold and glittering, Josh saw, but then the Raider cried out, "Take them! Do not kill them!"

At once the Raiders put away their bows, replaced their arrows, and came to the ground. Somehow, when they came their wings folded up neatly on their backs as an eagle's wings fold as he comes to his perch.

The leader landed lightly in front of Josh. He was very lean and not at all tall. There was not an ounce of surplus flesh on his body, although the muscles were clearly visible. He pulled a knife from his belt and said, "You're our prisoners. You're our slaves."

Josh did not answer for a moment. He was studying the man carefully. He saw at once that the wings were not a part of the man's body. The crossed belts across the man's chest held the apparatus in place. There were, he saw, some sort of cables, tiny, almost invisible, that ran down the legs and fastened at the ankle. Other cables ran down the arms and fastened around the wrist. He did not understand but saw that the cables were attached to the wings. Somehow these people had learned how to create artificial flight in a way that men on earth had always dreamed. He remembered suddenly that Leonardo da Vinci had devised a set of wings but had never proven them to be practical.

The leader had spoken in the dialect used all over Nuworld and understood by all people. Josh had learned it when he first came and now answered, "We come in peace to speak to your leader."

The Raider, who was dark complected and had a sneer on his face, laughed aloud. "The white one wants to speak to our leader!" he called out, and there was laughter among the other Raiders. He stepped forward and grabbed Josh's arm. His grip was paralyzing. He was stronger than any person his size had a right to be. He reached with his other hand and held Josh's face, his fingers clamping into the jaw. "You all have white skin, except that little one. You're not Desert People."

"No, we're the servants of Goél."

Instantly Josh saw that the word meant something to the Raider. He stiffened, and his grip grew tighter. "Goél? Goél is our enemy!" he snapped. "You'll discover that Goél has no power in the Citadel among the Raiders." A cruel smile crossed his lips. "My name is Darkwind. You shouldn't have come here, but I can promise that you will never leave."

For a moment Josh was unable to reply, for he'd seen that the name of Goél had raised some sort of hatred in Darkwind's dusky face. Then he said, "We mean no harm. We've come to help."

Darkwind laughed aloud. "You will help," he said. "We have need for many slaves." Then he said, "Come, we'll take them to the Citadel."

What happened next was startling. The Raiders began to produce ropes which they quickly lashed around the arms and legs and bodies of the Sleepers. Then four of them took one line apiece and sprang into the air. Their wings somehow spread through the system of cables and caught the breeze that was whipping over the desert. Instantly they began to rise. It was unlikely that any one of them could have picked up a Sleeper alone, but four of them together made a very powerful engine.

Josh felt himself snatched from the ground as the four that held him by the cords tied to his body began to rise. As they went higher, the breeze was stronger, so they rose even more rapidly.

Looking down, Josh saw Sarah snatched off the ground by four other Raiders. She cried out as the cords cut into her flesh, and Abigail was crying steadily. Reb had put up a fight, but he'd been knocked to the ground and tied fast and now he too was being lifted.

Soon they were high above the earth. Josh felt sick as the ground disappeared. He was totally helpless. He looked up at the glistening, dark bodies of the Raiders who carried him swiftly onward. They were cruel beings, he knew from their expressions. He looked ahead and saw the Citadel coming closer. They picked up speed, gliding into the wind, and he remembered suddenly the time the Sleepers had ridden on huge eagles to escape the power of the Sanhedrin.

Somehow he knew they were in worse trouble than they had ever been, and he murmured, "Goél, I may have gotten us into this, but I sure can't get us out."

Jake was silent as he looked down at the ground. He had never liked heights, and he certainly didn't like the faces of those who carried him. "Well," he said almost philosophically, "I hate to say I told you so, Josh, but I told you so!"

Josh, of course, was far away and couldn't hear, and Jake took no satisfaction in being right this time. He didn't like the looks of Darkwind's face, and the idea of being a slave frightened him. He set his jaw and thought about the times Goél had delivered them and shook his head. As the earth rushed beneath him, he thought, *It's going to be tough, but I know somehow we're going to make it.*

5

Lord of the Winged Ones

Jake found himself unceremoniously dumped on the rock floor of a spacious arena. He grunted as he struck the ground, protesting, "Hey! Watch it, you birds, you could break my neck!"

One of his guards, a wiry, dark-skinned raider, reached out and slapped him across the mouth. "Better be glad you didn't get worse," he snarled. "Watch your mouth, or we'll drop you over the side of the cliff!"

"Take it easy, Jake," Dave said. "Don't get these guys upset."

Jake had a fiery temper, but he realized that Dave was probably right. He kept quiet as his captors unfastened him and stood rubbing his arms where the ropes had bitten into them. Looking around, he saw they were in some sort of natural amphitheater. On one end was a raised shelf of solid rock and on it a throne built of some sort of horns all woven intricately together. On the throne sat a man, staring at the newcomers from a pair of dark, steady eyes.

"What have you brought back, Darkwind?" he called loudly.

Darkwind advanced two steps toward the throne and said, "Chief White Storm, we have had a good raid." Turning, he waved his hand toward the prisoners. "See, we have snared seven ripe young birds. They will make good slaves, though they are young."

The chief stared at the captives and nodded. "You are now the prisoners of the Winged Raiders," he said. "If you behave yourselves and give no trouble, you will find it much better."

Josh hesitated for one moment, then he stepped forward and held up his hand in a gesture of peace. "Chief White Storm," he said, "may I speak?"

Surprised at the sudden words of the captive, White Storm smiled, then nodded. "Yes," he said. "I am curious. Come closer." He waited until Josh was only a few feet away, then he rose from his throne. The wings that were so cleverly affixed to him nestled against his back leaving his arms free. He was no taller than Josh but was very strong and wiry, as were all of the Winged Raiders. His face was like that of a hawk, and there were scars on his cheeks and on his powerful chest and arms—old battle scars, Josh knew instantly.

"You are not part of the Desert People," he said. "Your skin is too light. All of you except that little dark one are already cooking under the sun. Who are you? Where are you from?"

"I am Josh Adams, and these are my friends." Josh quickly named the others. "We are called, by some, the Seven Sleepers."

A thought crossed the mind of the chief and was reflected in his eyes. "I have heard of Seven Sleepers," he said. "There is some sort of song that has come even as far as the Citadel."

"Yes," Josh said eagerly. "There is a song. It goes like this:

"The house of Goél will be filled,
The earth itself will quake!
The Beast will be forever stilled,
When Seven Sleepers wake!"

When Josh finished the song, he said, "We come in peace, Chief White Storm. We are the servants of Goél,

42

and we want to bring good will between the Winged Raiders and the Desert People."

Darkwind laughed loudly. "There will be peace," he said in a loud voice, "when the Desert People surrender to our rule and become our slaves."

"We do not believe in slavery, nor does Goél," Josh said sturdily.

White Storm was examining the captives. He shook his head, saying, "You do not understand our way of life. Look around you," he said. He waited until Josh's eyes had swept the barren, rocky terrain. Only here and there were there any signs of greenery, bushes struggling to keep life in the rocky terrain. "We live in a hard land. My people are hunters, but we must grow food. To do that, we must have slaves. That is why we raid the Desert People, so that we may survive."

"They must survive too," Josh spoke up. "We have been in many lands, Chief White Storm, and we have seen people come together instead of fighting."

"Do not listen to him," Darkwind cried out. "He is a spy sent to destroy our people. You well know the laws of our tribe, Chief White Storm. The captives we take are to be divided among our people. There is need for workers." He looked at the Sleepers with some contentment. "These are frail and will probably burn out after a few years of work, but it is our right to use them as long as they live."

A murmur of agreement went around the circle of Winged Raiders that surrounded the throne and the captives. Cries went up, "Yes, let us have the slaves!"

For one moment, Josh thought that Chief White Storm would deny the cries. Something like a grieved look swept across his face. He was obviously a man of war—yet there was more compassion in his visage than in that of Darkwind and the others. Finally, quiet fell across the arena, and Chief White Storm broke it by saying, "We must keep the laws of our people." He looked at the Sleepers. "As I said, you will make it difficult if you rebel. There is no way of escape from this place. Those who have tried have died." He pointed toward the sheer cliff. "Without wings you would fall and kill yourselves trying to get down from here. Obey your masters, and things will be easier for you." He rose from his throne and nodded toward an older man. "See that they are divided fairly among the warriors, Sure Flight."

"Yes, sir." The speaker was a bronzed warrior who stood to the right of the chief. He was somewhat larger than the other warriors and had a look of command about him. His hair was dark but had a reddish tint to it. He stood looking at the captives, then began to call out names. "You, Darkwind, can have the dark-skinned one," he said, indicating Wash. "He will not burn in the sun like the others and may last longer."

Wash gave Josh a look of despair. "I *would* get him!" he whispered. But there was no help for it. The warrior Darkwind approached, grabbed Wash by the wrist, and dragged him out, away from the crowd.

One by one, Sure Flight assigned the Sleepers to different warriors. Finally, Jake alone was left.

"You will come with me," he said.

Jake stared at him, his heart sinking. He could still hear the cries of Sarah as she had been dragged away by one of the Raiders, and he determined, no matter how bad things got, never to let a complaint pass his lips.

The crowd began to break up, and Jake followed Sure Flight down a rock trail that led past several caves hewn out of the solid rock. He passed one that was little more than an outline and saw one of the Winged Raiders observing four dark-skinned workers who were chipping away at the rock, seemingly making little progress.

Unable to restrain himself, Jake asked his captor, "Are they trying to make a cave?"

Sure Flight gave the small young man a swift look. "Yes. It will take a long time, but it must be done."

Jake had the dreadful thought that he might spend the rest of his life chipping away at solid rock under the blazing sun. He ducked his head against the whistling wind that was always present, and his head was already beginning to swim with thoughts about escape. He said nothing more to Sure Flight, however, and finally they arrived at a ladder that was leaning against a sheer face of rock. Ten feet up was the entrance to a cave, and Sure Flight motioned. "In there!"

Jake scrambled up the ladder and waited until the warrior had mounted behind him.

"In here," Sure Flight said briefly.

Inside the cave, Jake was surprised. This was not a handmade cave but one that had obviously been created by the action of wind. It had scoured a large cavern at least twelve feet high and in an irregular shape. Furniture was scattered around, and rugs were on the floor. Several small holes had evidently also been scoured out by the wind, allowing the sunlight to come in. To Jake's further surprise, it was cool inside, almost like an underground cave.

"Who is this?"

Jake was startled by a voice. He had thought the cave was empty. Now he turned quickly to his right and saw a young woman wearing a white tunic that came to her knees. She had the same features as Sure Flight, and her hair was even a more pronounced red than his. Even at this low point in his life, Jake had time to think, *She sure is a pretty girl!*

"This is my daughter, Lareen." Sure Flight turned to the girl and smiled fondly. "You won't have to work so hard now, daughter," he said. "Darkwind brought back seven captives, and this will be your slave."

"He's not very big," Lareen complained. She came forward and, to Jake's amazement, began to feel his arms and punch him in the chest. "Why, look how flabby he is, Father!" The girl sniffed, disdain in her voice. "If you put wings on him, he couldn't fly for a minute."

"He won't have wings." Sure Flight laughed. "That's the last thing any of our captives need. He can be taught to do the cleaning and some of the cooking. It will leave you more free time."

"I wish he were bigger," Lareen said with a frown. Then she brightened and said, "Thank you, Father. What's its name?"

"I'm not an *it!*" Jake burst out. "And my name is Jake Garfield." His red hair was ruffled from the windy flight, and his brown eyes were filled with anger.

Lareen laughed loudly. "Well, it can talk," she said. "But it will have to be taught manners." She walked over to the side the cave, searched for a moment, then came back with a small stick. Holding it up in front of Jake, she said, "Garfield, you see this?"

"I see it."

"It's for children and slaves who don't mind their masters." She held it in front of his nose, then tapped him on the forehead with it. "Don't make me use it."

Jake's face turned red, and an angry reply leaped to his lips. He was an independent, touchy young man, jealous of his rights. He was the more angry because he had advised against this mission and now felt that he had been ignored. For one moment the angry words that boiled inside him were almost spoken, but he happened to catch a glimpse of Sure Flight's face and, just in time, clamped his lips together.

46

Sure Flight had been watching him. Now he relaxed, and his lips bent upward at the corners into a smile. "Second thoughts are usually best, Garfield," he murmured. "If you obey me and my daughter, you will be treated well. If you do not, you will be beaten." He came over and stroked Lareen's hair. "I must go to a meeting of the council. Use Garfield as you will."

As soon as Sure Flight was out of the cave, Lareen held the stick lightly with one hand, stroking it with the other. Her eyes were large and almond shaped, and she had very thick lashes. Her skin was golden, and she had a well-shaped mouth. Her hair was long, falling almost to her waist. She had a curious expression on her face and said, "Before I put you to work, tell me who you are, Garfield. Where did you come from? I've never seen such white skin before."

Jake shrugged and gave an explanation of the Seven Sleepers to the girl, who listened carefully. He said finally, "We came to the Citadel to try to bring peace between the Raiders and the Desert People."

"That will never be."

"Why not?

"Why, because we're enemies. They would kill us in a minute if they could. It's always been that way," she said firmly.

Jake was annoyed by the simplicity of the answer. "It doesn't have to be like that. People can learn to trust each other, you know."

"I trust my father," Lareen said. "I trust Chief White Storm. I trust our people but no one else."

Jake had no answer for that. He was tired and terribly thirsty.

The girl evidently saw his parched lips and said, "Come this way." She led him around a corner of the room to a small area that had been hollowed out, by hand apparently.

"You will sleep here. This is where the slaves sleep." Then she turned and took him to a hollowed-out chunk of rock that stood in the shadows. "This will be your job," she said. She picked up a cup and handed it to him. "You will make sure that the water is brought here."

He took the cup and, when she said, "You may drink," he eagerly scooped some water into it and drank thirstily. He refilled the cup again and when he would have filled it a third time, she reached out and took the cup from him. "That's enough. You've already had your day's supply of water."

"That little cup—or two of them?" Jake exclaimed. "Why, I usually spill more than that!"

Lareen said, "You won't spill any here. Come, I'll show you what to do." She led him out of the cave and almost flew down the ladder, she was so agile.

Jake stumbled to keep up. Overhead from time to time there were winged men flying, sailing along on the breeze that always moaned or whistled on top of the plateau.

They walked for what seemed like a long time, headed downhill, and finally came to a part of the Citadel that had more light. Jake saw what looked to be a very large garden with half-naked slaves working among the small, green plants. "You will work some on the farm," Lareen said. "But now, I'll show you the water."

As Jake followed her he saw that the slaves were watering the small plants, each of them carrying a bucket or cup. They would dip out water and pour it carefully around the base of the root. It was a very primitive kind of irrigation system in which no water at all was wasted.

They reached a door guarded by two armed Raiders who eyed Jake suspiciously.

"This is our new slave. Its name is Garfield," Lareen said. "It will come to bring the water to our house."

When they nodded, she passed inside the cave. Instantly Jake felt the coolness. They walked down a slanting walkway for what seemed to be a long time. Candles set in holders furnished a flickering, feeble light. Finally Lareen stopped so suddenly that Jake ran into her. "Watch where you're going, Garfield!" she snapped.

Jake looked down and saw two more armed guards. They were outlined by torches set in the side of the wall, and at their feet was what appeared to be a well with a curbing.

"This is Garfield," Lareen said again. "It will bring the water for our house." She held out the two buckets that she had brought, and one of the guards sheathed his sword and let down a container on the rope. It seemed to take a long time, and Jake heard a faint splash far, far below. When the guard pulled it up, he very carefully measured out the water into the two buckets.

"You carry them," Lareen said to Jake and then turned and walked out.

Jake followed, and, by the time they had gotten to the entrance, the pails were cutting into the palms of his hands, but he said nothing.

"Come on, and don't spill one drop of that water," Lareen said. She led him quickly back to their cave and, when they got to the ladder, said, "Give me one of them." Taking the one bucket she scampered up the ladder and then waited for him.

She poured the contents of her bucket carefully into the stone reservoir and said, "Put the water in there."

When Jake had poured in the water she said, "Now, you can go back. Carry water until it is full."

Jake turned to go, but her voice caught him. "Stop, Garfield! When I speak to you, you will say, 'Yes, Mistress.' You will call my father 'Master.'" She watched him carefully, almost as if she hoped he would refuse.

But Jake shrugged and said, "Yes, Mistress," then picked up the buckets and walked out of the cave.

Carrying the water was tedious business. It took Jake ten trips to complete that task. He kept his eyes open, and once he saw Reb walk by carrying a heavy burden, led by a rather heavyset woman who scolded him in a shrill voice.

"I guess me and Reb both got women trouble," Jake muttered. Finally, he got back on the last trip, poured the last of the water into the reservoir, and said, "I'm glad that's over."

But Lareen, who had been sitting on a chair watching him, said, "Now! You can entertain me."

Jake stared at her. "Entertain you? What are you talking about—Mistress?" He added the last quickly when her eyes flashed.

Lareen said, "Can you sing?"

"Of course I can sing."

"Very well, sing me some of the songs of your people."

Jake was sorry that he had admitted that he was able to sing, and in truth he was not very good at it. But he saw that the girl was determined and began to sing one of the old Beatles songs from Oldworld.

Lareen listened to it, then said, "That's a good song, but you're not much of a singer." She began to sing herself, and Jake was shocked to hear what a good voice she had and that she had memorized the song just from hearing it once.

"You're a good singer," he said. "You'd need to go on a concert tour back in the old days."

"What's a concert tour?"

Jake explained basically what it had been, and Lareen's eyes glowed with pleasure. "I'd have liked that," she said. "Everybody listening to me and clapping their hands."

Jake was weary and said, "Is it all right if I sit down before I do anything else?"

Lareen said, "Come, I'm going to teach you how to cook."

Jake's heart sank, but he sat and watched as she prepared the meal. He was so tired that he fell asleep once, and finally Lareen said, "You're going to have to do better than that, Garfield. I won't have a slave around that goes to sleep."

"Yes, Mistress," Jake said wearily, then promptly closed his eyes and went to sleep out of sheer exhaustion.

6

Jake Takes a Chance

Two days after they were taken into captivity, Jake finally had a chance to speak with Reb. The two of them met at the well and, after filling their buckets, moved out of hearing range of the guards.

"How's it going, Reb?" Jake asked.

"Well, it ain't finer'n frog hair, I can tell you that!" Reb snapped. He turned his cheek to one side, and in the flickering light Jake saw a red mark.

"Who gave you that?"

"Doesn't matter," Reb said wearily. "I'm everybody's slave around there. If I don't hop when they say, they take a stick to me." He shrugged his shoulders wearily, saying, "We're in a mess for sure this time, Jake. I don't see how we can ever get out."

Jake almost reminded Reb that he had said the very same thing, but the weariness and the discouragement on his friend's face caused him to say instead, "We've been in tight spots before. We'll get out."

"Yeah, but it'll take a miracle," Reb said. "What's it like where you are?"

"Well, it could be worse, I guess. Sure Flight's the second-in-command. He seems to be a pretty nice fellow actually, aside from being a Raider—but it's that daughter of his that's giving me fits."

"Does she beat you?"

"Oh, she gives me a whack now and then just to show her authority," Jake grumbled. He thought about the past two days and how Lareen had kept at him constantly.

She was as curious as a girl could be, and, when Jake was so tired he could hardly stand up, she would prod him with the stick, forcing him to tell her more about his experiences in the outside world. She seemed to delight in tormenting him, and, while she was not cruel, she nearly drove him crazy with her demands.

"It could be worse." Jake shrugged, then asked, "Have you seen any of the others?"

"Yeah, I saw Abbey. She's about cried out, I reckon." Reb shook his head sadly. "Hard on a young girl like that. She said she saw Sarah, and the two of them are about as sad as we are about all of this."

"We'll get away." Jake nodded.

They had reached the surface now, and the guards passed them by.

When they came to the fork that separated their pathways, Reb looked out over the vast spaces where the desert land far below sent up heat spirals. The wind was whistling and blowing his pale bleached hair.

He was a tough young man, but somehow this had destroyed his confidence in himself. He said only, "Let's just try to get together. If they keep us separated like this, we'll lose all hope."

"Sure, we'll do that," Jake said quickly. He felt a pang as he watched Reb trudge away carrying his buckets and thought, *If Reb's downhearted, I don't know what'll happen. He's the toughest of us all.*

He was on his way back to the cave when he heard voices overhead. He saw two Winged Raiders standing on a ledge, peering out over the desert. He could not see their faces, but he recognized the voice of Darkwind.

"Nachor, I tell you, we've got to move quickly," Darkwind said. The whistling wind almost drowned out his voice, and Jake huddled close to the stone outcropping,

54

listening as hard as he could. Nachor said something that he could not catch, and then Darkwind spoke again. "We'll never be able to sway White Storm. He'll have to go."

This time Nachor's voice came to him more clearly. "You mean kill the chief?"

"Yes. Haven't you always known it would come to that? If we're going to join the Shadow Wings, White Storm can't stay."

Nachor was silent for a moment, then asked, "What about Sure Flight? He's totally loyal to White Storm."

"He'll have to go too, and any others that won't go our way."

"I'm not sure we're strong enough. There's only a few of us, and if they find out we are in league with the Shadow Wings, they'll strip our wings and throw us over the edge of the cliff to die."

"There are powers that you do not know, Nachor," Darkwind said and laughed in a sinister fashion. "We will talk of this later. Come, let's make our patrol."

Instantly Jake pressed himself against the outcropping, trying to freeze as the two Raiders threw themselves off into the wind. Their wings spread, and they caught the wind at once, rising high. Once Jake thought that Darkwind glanced down and saw him, but he remained absolutely still. Finally he drew a deep breath as the two forms rose high into the air, becoming mere black dots as they sailed out over the desert land.

"Whew! That was a close one!" Jake said, his voice not quite steady. He hurried on back toward the cave of Sure Flight, his mind filled with what he had heard.

"There's some kind of plot going on," he said to himself. "The Shadow Wings—that sounds like servants of the Dark Lord to me. He's got his spies *here*."

When he reached the cave, he found Lareen waiting with her stick. She prodded him with it, something she knew he hated, saying, "You took too long. Come, put the water in the reservoir. We have things to do."

Jake did as she indicated, then followed her out of the cave. She took him to a part of the village that he had not seen before. A group of women were working in the shade, and Jake said, "Look! They're making wings!"

"Of course they're making wings. That's what they do."

Jake said, "Let me take a look."

Lareen glanced at him, then shrugged. "All right, for just a minute."

Jake moved over and saw that making wings was an intricate process. He did not know what the framework was. He suspected some sort of metal that they had brought back from raids, but it was very, very light. The women were attaching individual feathers with tiny threads. It was a painstaking, slow process.

Lareen picked up a wing that was half done and held it toward Jake. "See, this is what makes our people kings of the desert. You've never seen anything like this, have you?"

Jake took the wing and noted it was made of literally thousands of tiny feathers, all tied in layers. It was very light and yet somehow flexible. It bent and moved easily.

"That's enough," Lareen snapped. "Come on now."

Jake followed her obediently but asked, "Why don't *you* wear wings? Don't any of the women fly?"

"Of course! Don't be so stupid," Lareen snapped. "Only the best of us women get to fly."

"I don't see why a woman couldn't fly as well as a man," Jake observed.

Instantly Lareen turned to him and opened her eyes wide. That seemed to be a new thought to her. She stood there thinking hard. Then finally she shrugged her shoulders. "Well, you're right about that, but lots of things aren't fair, I guess."

The two passed out of the central part of the village past the farm, coming finally to what was the closest thing to a forest. It wasn't much, Jake saw. Seeds had taken root in the crevices of the rocks, and a thin soil had been built up. Some of the trees were ten feet high, or even fifteen.

"We need to gather firewood," Lareen said. "Don't hurt any of the trees."

Jake began to pick up small dead sticks, putting them into the sack that Lareen had tossed him. As he worked, she sat in the shade of one of the trees singing a song that he had never heard before.

Then she rose and looked around and said, "There! You've missed that big pile of dry wood over there. Come on."

Lareen walked toward the pile of wood, and Jake followed. She reached it and turned to say, "Now, put all this in your sack and we'll go home."

Just as she finished speaking, she whirled her head, and Jake saw her lips open in a soundless scream. He glanced down and saw a coiled snake almost at her feet. The girl seemed paralyzed, unable to move, and the snake was drawing back for its strike.

Without thinking, Jake dropped the sack of sticks and threw himself forward. He shoved Lareen to one side and tried to roll away, but he was too late.

He cried out as the fangs of the snake struck him on the calf of his right leg. At the same time, he picked up a stick and hit the reptile behind the head. The snake began to writhe, and Jake struck again and again until finally it lay still. He stood there, trembling, and looked down at the two fang marks on his leg.

Lareen had fallen, but she got to her feet and came to him. Her face seemed to be frozen, and she was trembling violently. "He bit you!" she whispered.

"Yes, he did," Jake managed to say.

At once she said, "Quick, lie down."

Jake lay down on the thin soil. He saw Lareen remove the dagger from her belt, and he stared at her as she approached.

"The snake is deadly," Lareen whispered. "I must cut the wound."

"Go ahead," Jake said, gritting his teeth. He looked away and felt her hand on his leg. Then there was a quick flash of pain as the blade bit into his leg. He felt it again on the other fang mark and then felt her hands kneading his flesh. He felt the blood run down the calf of his leg and asked, "Do people—die when these things bite them?"

When Lareen leaned over him, her lips were pale and held in a tight line. Slowly she nodded. "Sometimes they do, but not always. You lie here; don't move. I'll go get help."

She was gone then, and Jake lay there looking up at the sky. He seemed to hear his heart beating, thudding like a drum, and his body felt hot. Soon he became very sick, but he lay still. Finally he whispered, "Well, Goél, if this is it, it's been good to serve you."

* * *

"I think he's going to be all right."

Jake had been asleep in a dark pit, it seemed, but he came back. When he opened his eyes, everything was wavering for a minute. The yellow light of a flickering torch cast its gleam over faces. They were blurred, and he blinked his eyes. When he opened them again, he saw it was Sure Flight and Lareen, along with an older man.

58

"What—where am I?" Jake tried to speak, but his lips were dry.

The old man at once turned to him. "Don't try to talk. You've been very sick."

Jake felt terrible. His head ached, and it seemed as if every bone in his body had been broken.

"You'll feel better after a while." This was Lareen, who came to stand beside him, putting her hand on his forehead.

Jake licked his lips, then grinned feebly. "That's good. I'd hate to think I'd feel this bad the rest of my life."

Sure Flight leaned over the young man, his face very serious. "I'm glad you did not die, Garfield. My daughter has told me what you did for her. It was a brave thing to do."

Jake could not remember for a moment what had happened. His mind was whirling, and then finally he did remember taking the snakebite. His mind was foggy, and he said, "Jake Garfield's Maiden Rescue Service. We never close."

Lareen whispered, "I'm terrified of snakes. I couldn't move."

"Well, I don't care much for them myself," Jake said.

He tried to sit up, but the old man pushed him down. His name was Lochor, they said, and he was the nearest thing these people had to a doctor as Jake was to discover. "Lie still," he said. "You must eat and rest for two days."

That was the way it turned out. After the first day, Jake was much better, but Lareen insisted on his lying very still. She cooked broth for him and insisted on serving him.

Once Sure Flight saw her feeding Jake the broth and smiled. "It looks like the slave and the mistress have changed positions," he observed.

Lareen flushed but made no answer. When her father was gone, she put the bowl down and said, "How do you feel?"

Jake nodded. "A lot better than I did." He gave her an odd look. "You treat all your slaves like this?"

"Not all my slaves risk their lives to save mine," Lareen said. "Why did you do it?"

Jake was embarrassed. "I didn't stop to think about it." He shrugged. "When you see a snake, you do all you can to keep it from biting somebody. Then you kill it."

"I could never have done that." There was an almost pathetic look on the beautiful face of the young woman. She said, "You're different from us, Garfield. Most of my people would not have done that. My father would. Maybe a few more."

Jake said suddenly, "I think it's because I serve Goél."

"Who *is* Goél? I've heard of him, but I know nothing of him."

Jake thought of the plot he had overheard on the rocks and thought, *I'd better begin making some converts to Goél's way or we're all goners.* Aloud he said, "Goél is good. There's a dark power that lives in Nuworld. There are cruel people who would hurt others. Goél would have everyone to be kind and generous—as you've been to me lately," he concluded suddenly.

Lareen flushed but continued to ask questions about Goél.

Jake answered them, then asked cautiously, "Have you ever heard of the Shadow Wings?"

Lareen gave him a startled look, "Yes. They're a small tribe that lives far away. They have been here several times."

"Your people don't get along with the Shadow Wings?"

"Some do." Lareen nodded slowly. "But my father thinks it would be foolish to make an alliance with them.

He has spoken with Chief White Storm about this many times."

"But Darkwind doesn't agree, does he?"

"How do you know that?"

Jake shrugged. "Oh, just a guess." He hesitated, then said, "I hope your father and the chief don't get involved with these Shadow Wings. They're not like your people, not if they're the servants of the Dark Lord."

For a long time the two sat there talking, and finally Lareen rose. She put out her hand, and impulsively Jake took it. "You saved my life, Garfield," she said. "I will never forget. Can I do anything for you?"

Jake grinned crookedly at her. "Well, one thing. Please don't hit me with that stick again!"

7

A New Chance

For two more days Jake found himself practically an invalid. The venom of the serpent had been worse than he had imagined, and he was so weak that he could barely feed himself. Lareen kept close watch over him, and her father, Sure Flight, stopped by from time to time to inquire in a kindly fashion about his condition.

On the third day, Jake managed to get to his feet and take a few tottering steps. He was dizzy, and his legs felt as though they were made out of rubber. Just as he was about to make his way back to his bed, a young man came through the cave opening and startled him.

"Who are *you?*" the young man demanded. He was no more than seventeen or so, trim and wearing the wings of a raider. His eyes were dark, as was his hair, and there was a look of authority about him.

"My name's Jake Garfield. Who are *you?*"

The question seemed to irritate the young man, but he answered, "I am Swiftwind, son of Chief White Storm." He examined Jake with a rather suspicious glance, then demanded, "Where is Lareen?"

Jake's legs were getting even more shaky, and his dizziness increased. "I don't know where she is," he muttered.

The young man called Swiftwind seemed to take his mutter as an insult. He reached out and struck Jake across the chest. Ordinarily the blow would not have disturbed Jake, but in his weakness it was enough to drive him backward. He sprawled on the hard stone floor, and his head rapped the surface. It sent stars flashing across his eyes, and for one moment he seemed to lose consciousness. When he awoke, it was only a few moments later, but he heard voices and felt hands on his head.

"Who do you think you are?"

Jake opened his eyes and saw Lareen, bending over him and holding his head off the floor. She was glaring at the young man Swiftwind and proceeded to give him a dressing down. "If you can't behave any better than that, Swiftwind, you can just take yourself out of here!"

The young man looked sheepish. "But, Lareen—"

"Never mind." Lareen helped Jake get to his feet, and he slumped over on the couch that was built into the wall. "Are you all right, Jake?" she asked anxiously.

Jake felt the back of his head, which had a slight swelling, but nodded. "Yes, I'm all right. Not much stronger than a baby though."

Lareen turned to Swiftwind, her eyes flashing. "I suppose you're proud of yourself, pushing an invalid around. You're a real son of a chief, you are! Why don't you go out and find some babies and whip on them?"

"Wait a minute," Swiftwind protested. "I didn't hit him that hard—and I didn't know he was sick. Who is he anyway?"

"He's one of the captives that Darkwind brought in five days ago. I was about to be bitten by a snake, and it was Jake who jumped between me and the awful thing. He took the bite in his leg that would have been mine." She glared at Swiftwind and snapped, "I'm not sure anyone else would have done that."

Jake watched as they faced each other. It occurred to him that perhaps Swiftwind had come courting Lareen. He wanted to make no trouble. "Wait a minute, Mistress," he said. "I'm sure Swiftwind didn't mean any harm, and he didn't really hit me that hard. I'm just not very strong yet."

64

Eagerly Swiftwind said, "That's right. Sorry about that." He glanced at Lareen and laughed sheepishly. "I never thought I'd hear myself apologizing to a slave—but sometimes my temper does get away from me."

Lareen seemed to relent. "All right," she said. "Now, sit down and tell me everything you've been doing."

Jake listened carefully as Swiftwind began to describe his adventures. He was seventeen years old, as Jake had suspected, and was beginning his training with the more adventurous arm of the Raider branch. They made long sweeps over the desert, looking for plunder and slaves. As he spoke he grew more excited. Finally he looked at Jake and asked, "Why are you so white? You look like you'd burn up out in the sun."

Jake, who did as a matter of fact burn easily, nodded. "That's right, but in the country I come from the sun isn't as hot as it is here. As a matter of fact, some places are covered with ice."

"What is 'ice'?" Swiftwind asked curiously.

Jake tried to explain ice, but to the two young people who had never seen anything like that, the explaining was a total failure.

"You mean you're telling me you can actually walk on water?" Lareen asked, doubt in her eyes.

"Well, it's just not like it is here," Jake said. "I know it sounds like a big lie, but that's the way it is in part of this world."

As the three young people were talking, Lareen's father walked in through the opening of the cave.

"Well, you're back from your mission, Swiftwind," he said. "I hope it went well."

"Very well." Swiftwind nodded. He hesitated, then said, "We saw some of the Shadow Wings in the sweep over to the south."

At once Sure Flight's face clouded. "Did you talk with any of them?"

"Darkwind did. He was leading the mission." A frown came to Swiftwind's face, and he shook his head. "He had a parley with their leaders, but I don't know what they said."

At once Jake thought of the conversation he had heard between Darkwind and the other raider. He thought to mention it but didn't want to appear to be a spy.

The two men talked for a while, and from their conversation Jake learned they were very suspicious of the Dark Lord. Finally Sure Flight turned to Jake and said, "I've been thinking much about your leader, Goél. Tell me more about him."

Eagerly Jake began to explain the powers of Goél. It was difficult for him, because he could not say for certain that Goél had sent them here. But the best he could, he told some of their past adventures, how Goél had led them to defeat the powers of the Dark Lord and of the Sanhedrin. At last he said, "All of Nuworld is under some kind of attack, sir. Everywhere we Sleepers go, we find some who believe in Goél. But others have become slaves to the Dark Lord."

"That's what I've always felt." Swiftwind nodded. "I think we ought to be more careful."

"I've tried to talk with your father," Sure Flight said slowly. "He's coming around, but he still listens to Darkwind." Then he turned to Jake and seemed to put the matter away. "I have good news for you."

Jake grinned suddenly. "Well, I could use some, sir. What is it?"

"I went to the chief and told him what you did for my daughter. He was quite impressed, and he was feeling very lenient, I think. So I asked a favor of him."

"What was it, Father?" Lareen asked eagerly.

66

"I told him that by your act of courage you had merited some reward, and he agreed. We talked for a long time, and finally I persuaded him to do something that has never been done."

For one instant Jake thought that Lareen's father had negotiated freedom for the Seven Sleepers. But then he knew that that could not be true. "I'd appreciate anything. All of us will," he said quickly.

"Well, I persuaded him that it would be good to treat all of you better. So what we're going to do is let you learn how to fly." He continued quickly, holding up his hand, "The chief said at once that it can't be done."

"I think he's right," Swiftwind said slowly. "Most of us start when we're four or five years old. They may be too old and their muscles too weak to control the wings."

"That may be," Sure Flight said, "but in any case, the chief agreed to let them try." He looked at Jake and studied him carefully. "If any of you do learn to master the wings, it may be that we can admit you to the fellowship of the Raiders. That too has never happened before," he observed, "and I think it unlikely, but at least you have a chance."

Jake thought about launching himself off a cliff such as the Citadel with nothing but a few feathers and had to swallow hard. He was not particularly fond of heights in the first place. However, he saw at once the possibilities of escape. *If we had wings,* he thought, *we could get away easily.* Aloud he said eagerly, "Thank you, sir. We'll do our best."

Sure Flight left soon afterward, taking Swiftwind with him.

At once Lareen said, "Oh, that's wonderful, isn't it, Garfield! And I can teach you so much. We'll start as soon as you're strong enough."

Jake managed to smile. "I hate to tell you this, Mistress, but . . . well . . . I never was good at getting up on high things."

"That's because you never had wings." Lareen nodded. "You were afraid you'd fall, but with wings you can soar like a bird."

"Well," Jake said slowly, "I'm willing to try if you'll help me." He looked over at the young girl and asked, "You like Swiftwind pretty well, don't you?"

Lareen shot him an embarrassed glance, and her face turned red. "He thinks he's really somebody," she muttered.

"Well, he *is* somebody! He's the chief's son, isn't he?" Jake teased her a little. "I bet lots of young girls would be tickled pink if he would come courting."

"What is courting?" she asked.

"That's when a young man comes calling on a young girl. Sometimes he brings her flowers and candy."

"Candy? What is candy?"

Jake spent the next half hour trying to explain courtship to Lareen, but in the end she shook her head. "The first thing is to teach you how to fly, Garfield. Come on, let's go pick out a pair of wings for you."

8
On Wings As Eagles

This sure beats hacking rock, don't it now?"

Reb looked over with satisfaction toward Wash. The two boys had been quick to answer the summons that had come. Both had simply been told they would be relieved from their duties for a while. Now, as they found their way to the spot where the others were gathered, Wash sighed deeply with satisfaction. "It sure does, Reb. I thought I knew what work was, but I guess I'm just really beginning to find out."

They joined the other five Sleepers, standing with a young woman and a young man of about seventeen on a slope that ran rather gently downhill.

"Hello, Reb," Josh said, "and you too, Wash." He gave them both a quick smile. "I hate to pull you away from your work, but I thought you might enjoy this."

"What's going on?" Reb demanded. He gave the young woman a careful look, then shifted his eyes to the winged warrior. "I don't mind telling you, I'm glad to be here."

"This is Lareen, the daughter of Sure Flight. He's the chief lieutenant of Chief White Storm. And this is Swiftwind. He's the son of the chief." Then Josh said, "Here's the deal. Jake here has proved himself to be a blooming hero."

Sarah interrupted, "Yes, he has, and I think we owe him a vote of thanks for that. I mean, he didn't want to come here in the first place."

"A hero?" Reb asked. He laid his pale blue eyes on

Jake and snorted, "The most heroic thing I ever saw him do is eat."

"Well, he did do something," Lareen spoke up quickly. She related how Jake had saved her life, and then her eyes sparkled, and she said, "And my father went to the chief. As a reward you're all going to be given a chance to become full-fledged members of the tribe."

"Well, how do we do that? Sign a pledge card?" Wash asked.

"No," Jake spoke up, his eyes glinting with amusement. "All you have to do is learn to fly."

"Fly?" Josh blinked with shock, and Reb was quiet too, stunned with the thought.

"What do you mean? With these wings?" Wash demanded.

"Well, they're not going to give us a Cherokee airplane," Josh said emphatically. "I guess at this point I'll have to say I'm grateful to Jake—but I'm not sure any of us will be able to master this thing. It looks pretty tough to me."

Jake spoke, "Aw, we can do it. Come on, Mistress Lareen, just show us how."

Lareen and Swiftwind gave each other an amused glance. They had learned that Jake would try practically anything.

Swiftwind said, "Anybody that'll tackle a snake can learn to fly. Why don't you show them how, Lareen, then I'll give them a little demonstration when you finish."

Lareen said at once, "All right. Come, I'll show you how it works." She led them over to a level spot where a large table and several chests rested on the stony floor. Opening one of the chests, she pulled out a pair of wings and said, "These are mine. Let me show you how to put them on."

70

The Sleepers watched carefully as Lareen began to don the wings. It was not as simple as it looked. Basically, the wings were joined together at the center and fastened to the body by two straps that crossed over the chest. That, however, was only the first step. An intricate system of tiny cables had to be carefully threaded along the limbs and fastened on the ankles, down the arms, and around the waist. Lareen put it on quickly, but they could all see it had taken long practice.

"Now," she said, "the wings are folded against my back, you see?" She turned around to show them. "But when I move this cable, they unfold." She gave her body a slight twist—very slight, and suddenly the wings that had been folded like a bird's spread out so that they were at least fifteen feet from wing tip to wing tip. "When they're spread out like this, they catch the wind, you see."

"Well, what are those other cables for?" Jake asked.

"Oh, all sorts of things," Lareen said. "Some move the feathers set in the trailing part of the wing so that they move up and down. That way, you can control them better."

"Can you do it without using your hands?" Sarah asked.

"Oh, yes—it wouldn't do much good to fly if you didn't have your hands."

"That's right," Swiftwind spoke up. "Learning to fly is only the first thing. You've got to learn to shoot a bow or use your sword or throw a spear at the same time you're flying."

Abigail shook her head. "I would never learn how to do all those things at the same time. Why, I can't even pat my head and rub my stomach at the same time."

Lareen looked at her curiously. "Why in the world would you want to do a thing like that?" Then she shrugged her shoulders, for she had learned that the Sleepers had odd ideas. "First things first," she said. "I'm going to take just a little flight, nothing fancy. You watch carefully. As I leap into the air, I'll spread the wings. There's a nice breeze, you see. If I do it right, it'll pick me up, and I'll begin to rise. Watch now."

The young woman had the wings folded. She took two or three short steps and threw herself forward. At the same time she pulled at the cables with her body so that the wings shot out. Instantly they caught the breeze. Her body was drawn into a diving position parallel with the ground, and at once the huge wings began to lift her up.

"See!" she cried out, "It's easy!"

Josh watched the girl sail gracefully through the air for about a hundred yards.

Then her voice came back, "See, I'm turning now, dropping one wing and raising the other."

Josh stared at her and whispered to Sarah, "Kinda like a hang glider when you think of it that way."

But Sarah shook her head. "It's more complicated than that. I don't think any of us will ever learn."

Lareen came back and said, "Now, that's how it's done. Swiftwind, you show them some of the more difficult things."

"All right." Swiftwind threw himself in the air, his wings spread, and he rose up swiftly. His wings were much larger than Lareen's, both in width and depth.

Josh was able to see that by means of the cables the wings moved almost as if they had life of their own. "Look at that," he muttered to Sarah.

They watched as the young man practically turned flips. He made abrupt turns, rose as if on a huge elevation. Then suddenly, when he was high in the air, he folded his wings and headed straight for the earth. When he was only a few hundred feet away, the wings spread and he made a swooping recovery, coming to light at their feet and folding the wings as he did so. He white teeth showed as he smiled pleasantly. "There! That's all there is to it. Who wants to try it?"

"Not me!" Wash said. "I get dizzy when I step up on a curb."

"What's a curb?" Swiftwind demanded, then shook his head. "Never mind. Lareen, you do your best. I've got to go on a mission. Teach them the fundamentals." He leaped into the air and soared away.

"That sure is a neat way to get from one place to another," Dave said as he watched Swiftwind disappear. Then he added doubtfully, "But if something goes wrong, he's got a long way to fall."

* * *

As the days went by, almost all the Sleepers despaired. For the first few days they did nothing but learn how to put on the wings. "Most of these are old and pretty worn out," Lareen had said. "It takes a long time to make wings. I don't know how many thousands of feathers and seams go into them," she admitted. "But they'll do for now."

"I don't think I'll ever learn how to judge the wind," Josh said ruefully. That was one of their hardest subjects, learning wind currents. They learned that there was an updraft under certain conditions and also downdrafts. So they had to study at least theoretically how to catch the updrafts.

"This is probably the only spot in the world where this kind of thing would work," Jake said to Josh one day as they were going over their lessons. "I don't know many places in Oldworld where the wind blew *all* the time."

"That's probably right," Josh admitted. He looked out over the wide sweep of terrain, noting how the land fell far away and the desert floor was so far away that the sheep below looked like tiny white dots. Carefully he walked to the edge, stared down, then turned back. "I don't think I'll ever be able to jump off this thing."

"Well, we've just got to, Josh! It may be our only way of getting out of this place. We can't climb down. The only way anybody ever leaves here is to fly."

"I supposed that's right." Josh shook his head. "But we haven't done a thing toward our mission. I guess I was wrong to lead us here, and you were right after all."

It was what Jake had been wanting to hear, but now that it came he did not seem particularly pleased. "Well, I don't know about that," he mumbled. "We'll just have to see."

Josh gave him a sharp look. "What are you thinking, Jake?"

"Well, there's something going on between the Raiders here and the Shadow Wings. That's the other tribe we've heard about far off to the north. From what I hear, they come straight from the Dark Lord himself. I've been trying to talk to Swiftwind about it, and he feels kinda the same way."

Josh grew excited. "Maybe *that's* why we came," he exclaimed, "—to do something to save these people from falling into the power of the Dark Lord!"

"Yeah, well, we can't save 'em while we're slaves." Jake shrugged. "So let's learn the best we can."

It was a week later that the seven were all gathered together on the slope, listening to Lareen explain more about flying. A sudden twinkle came into her eye, and she said, "Well, I think it's time to see what you've learned. Who'll be first?"

A silence fell over the group, and she laughed. "That's the quietest I've heard any of you. Come on, let's have a volunteer."

Dave spoke up, "Wash, you're the smallest and the youngest, and I think you ought to try first."

"What kind of thinking is that? You're the oldest and the biggest, so you ought to try."

An argument ensued, and finally Reb urged, "Go on, Wash, you can do it."

The others joined in, and finally Wash agreed reluctantly. He put on his wings and then said, as he stood there, "I feel like a buzzard."

"You'll do fine," Lareen said. "Now, we've gone over it a dozen times. Just throw yourself forward and spread your wings."

The others watched eagerly.

Wash took a deep breath and then began to run. He leaped into the air but evidently had not mastered the art of spreading the wings. One of them popped out, the wind caught it, and he began to spin in the air like a corkscrew. He hit the ground, and the dust puffed up. The others ran to him, and Reb pulled him to his feet. "Are you all right, Wash?"

"Oh, yeah, I'm all right," Wash said disgustedly, "but I don't think I'll ever learn how to fly."

"We all had falls. That's just like learning anything," Lareen said.

"Sure," Jake said, "it's like riding a bicycle."

"What's a bicycle?" Lareen asked.

When he told her, she said, "Wings are much better. Come on, Jake. I want you to try it next."

Jake stared at her, then nodded. "All right, I'll give 'er a try."

He put the wings on, got a few last-minute instructions, then said, "Well, here goes nothing." He made a longer run than Wash had and, trying to remember everything at once, flung himself into the wind. He did manage to get the wings open, and suddenly a thrill shot through him. "Look! I'm flying!" he hollered. He felt the wind lifting him, and the ground fell away in an alarming fashion. "Hey! How do I stop?" he yelled.

Lareen yelled a few instructions, and awkwardly Jake hauled at the wings. He went into a dive and heard Sarah screaming, "Come out of it, Jake!"

At the last minute he managed to spread the wings again and hit with a dull thud. He rolled in the dirt and got up in disgust, but the others were cheering.

"You did fine! Fine!" Josh said. "I hope the rest of us do that well."

"Yes, you did very well," Lareen said. Her eyes were shining, and she said, "Now, try it again. This time, I'll go with you and call out some instructions."

This time the two of them left the earth, Lareen gracefully and Jake still floundering, trying to do everything at once. "That's fine, Garfield," Lareen said, calling out instructions. "Now, let's just make a long glide." She hovered over him, explaining what to do, and Jake found to his delight that he was able to maintain a steady flight. "Now, we're going to turn," she said. "Remember the cable's on the right—twist your body."

Jake did as he was told and found to his surprise that he was turning. "I'm doing it! I'm doing it!" he yelled. "Look at me! I'm flying!"

The two came back to where the others were standing, and there was loud applause from the Sleepers.

"Well, that proves that one of us can learn anyway," Josh said. He looked a little pale but said, "Now, let me try."

All day they practiced, and, sooner or later, all of them made a successful flight, even Wash. It took all of them to convince Abigail to even try. But to her surprise, being so small, she found she could stay aloft easily. She was not afraid of heights as some of the others were and made good progress.

Sarah did not fare as well and took several hard falls.

Josh ran to her once and pulled her to her feet. "That was a tough one," he said. "Are you all right?"

Sarah wanted to just rest in his arms and say, "I'm through with this," but she knew she could not. "Yes, I'm all right. Let me try it again."

When they finished their lessons that day, Lareen said proudly, "You've all done well. Another week of fundamentals and you'll all be flying like birds."

Later, when she and Jake arrived at the cave, she said warmly, "Garfield, you did very well. Maybe someday you'll be a full-fledged warrior. Maybe even a chief."

"I'm too little for that." Jake shrugged.

"You think size is all that counts in a man? No," she said, "courage is what counts. If you have that, it doesn't matter how big you are."

Jake stared at her and said, with a smile, "Well, Mistress, I guess it's time for me to fix your supper."

"No, we'll fix it together," Lareen said. She smiled at him warmly, and suddenly Jake felt good all over. The two of them enjoyed their meal. Finally, afterward, he taught her some more songs, and she sang them back to him almost as if she were a tape recorder. When he mentioned this, she asked at once, "What's a tape recorder?"

Jake stared at her, then shrugged. "Just another useless invention I used to have," he said.

9

The Dark Lord Awakes

lmas, Chief Interrogator of the Sanhedrin, stood before a large map examining various marks in the form
of small black crosses. From time to time a look of satisfaction gleamed in his small eyes, and his lips curled upward in a ruthless smile. His office was circular, studded
with torches that cast a flickering glow over the thick form
of the Chief Interrogator.

Back in the shadows a dark form lurked. This was
Malon, the lieutenant of Elmas. He had learned long ago
to read the countenance of his chief, and when the brow of
the thickset figure wrinkled, he flinched slightly.

"What is it, Sire?" he asked quickly.

Elmas turned and put a baleful stare on Malon. "We
are not making enough progress," he grunted. His face
was fat and creased with thick folds, and there was an
elephantine clumsiness in him as he suddenly slapped the
wall with his fist. "Goél's forces seem to be surviving. I
want them stamped out!"

"But, Sire, we have slain many in the past weeks—"

"I don't want many, I want *all* of them dead. Why
didn't you—"

The stone door slid to one side, its rollers creaking,
and a red-robed figure came in quickly. "Sire," he said,
"you are summoned to the castle of the Dark Lord."

The face of Elmas was pale in any case, but it grew
even more pasty at this word.

"What did he say exactly?"

"Just for you to come quickly."

Elmas pulled himself together. Reaching toward a hook he withdrew a cape, threw it about his shoulders, and left his office. A journey to the castle of the Dark Lord was not a pleasant thing to contemplate. He settled himself inside his private carriage, and the horses began driving forward as he commanded the coachman, "Be quick to the castle!"

The horse hooves thundered over the road, and the carriage swayed from side to side. As the miles rolled by, Elmas sat hunched inside, wondering what would be awaiting him when he arrived. He was not a man without courage, but a visit to the Dark Lord always seemed to drain him of all strength.

It was growing dark when the carriage pulled up in front of the castle, a rising stone structure without ornament that seemed to cover the sky as he dismounted from his carriage. Ignoring the coachman, he advanced toward the door, which was a steel grate. A dark-cloaked warrior appeared from nowhere and cried, "What is your business?"

"The Dark Lord commands my presence. I am Elmas, Chief Interrogator of the Sanhedrin."

"Enter."

At the word, the gate rose creaking and grinding. The screech of its passage grated on the nerves of Elmas, and as he passed under he saw the sharp teeth along the lower edge and shivered to think what it would be like to be caught under them. He passed over a moat and, looking down, saw the waters stir with long, serpentine forms. Once a head emerged, filled with what seemed to be hundreds of razor sharp teeth. He shuddered, drew his cloak about him, and passed quickly over.

He was intercepted by another guard, who took him at once down a series of labyrinthine passageways. He passed many cell doors, and from some of them he heard the pitiful crying of the victims imprisoned inside. Once again he wished that he were anywhere except in the service of the Dark Lord. It paid well, but it was dangerous work!

"Wait here."

As the guard left him outside a huge door, guarded by four stalwart ruffians, Elmas thought, *I see now how little power I have. I make men tremble with my commands, but when the Dark Lord calls, it is I who am filled with terror.*

His guard reappeared, motioned silently, and stepped aside.

Elmas entered the room filled with memories of other visits. It was an enormous room with a cathedral ceiling, and torches lit the gloom, casting flickering shadows over a huge table that was big enough to seat a hundred men. The walls were draped with black, all bearing a strange silver device like a broken cross. At one end sat a throne on an elevated dais.

On the throne, a figure sat. The Dark Lord wore a black cloak with a hood that covered his features. Nevertheless, Elmas could see the burning red eyes that glittered in the murky darkness.

"Come closer, fool."

Elmas moved forward, his knees feeling weak as water. He fell on them at once, bowed, and said, "I come at your command, Most Dread Lord."

Silence filled the room, and Elmas was afraid to look up. Finally he lifted his eyes, and as he did the Dark Lord said, "As usual, you have failed. I do not know why I have allowed you to live so long."

"If Your Majesty will be more specific—"

"*I speak of the Seven Sleepers!*" The Dark Lord rose and came down the steps. He was tall and forbidding, and the hand that extended from the robe was strong and like an eagle's talon. Lifting one arm, he cried, "I have commanded you to kill them all, and you have failed!"

The hand closed around Elmas's throat. He felt the air leaving his body and cried out in a gurgling plea, "Stop! Please! Your Majesty!" The air seemed to grow hot, and he fell forward on his face, gagging and choking.

The tall figure slowly let his hand drop and waited until Elmas was able to sit up. "You have failed me, but the others are even bigger fools. I have word of the Seven Sleepers."

Elmas got to his feet shakily, and his voice quavered as he said, "Tell me where they are, Sire."

"Little good it will do. You always fail where they are concerned." Nevertheless, the Dark Lord turned to say, "They are in the desert country at a place called the Citadel."

"Yes, Sire, I know the place. I will send at once to have them killed."

"You have sent before and never have found them."

"This time we will not fail, Your Majesty." Elmas spoke with more assurance than he felt. Somehow, when the Seven Sleepers were mentioned, he always felt a quake of fear. He well knew the prophecies that, when the Seven Sleepers woke, the darkness would be rolled back. Nevertheless, he knew better than to speak his thoughts before the Dark Lord. Instead he said, "I have one who knows that country. His name is Jalor, and he was chief of the Shadow Wings before I sent him on an undercover mission to the Winged Raiders. He is acting as my spy there even as we speak."

"Then use him. Many of the Shadow Wings are fierce warriors. Surely they can kill seven children."

"Yes, Sire, I will go at once, if there is nothing else."

The Dark Lord nodded and gestured with imperial disgust. "Get out! And see that you do not fail."

Elmas scrambled to his feet and moved backward, bowing as he went. Finally he turned, and the door slammed shut behind him. He drew a shaking hand across his forehead, then glanced up to see the guards grinning at him. With a grunt he drew his robe about him and stalked out of the room. His guard was waiting, and then he was in his carriage headed back for the home of the Sanhedrin.

As soon as he arrived, he commanded, "Send word to Jalor that I must speak with him."

"Yes, Sire, at once!"

Two days later the door opened, and a red-robed priest announced, "Jalor—my lord Elmas."

A small man entered and stood before the Chief Interrogator. "You sent for me, my lord?" he asked. He was undersized, yet there was strength in his trim body. He had hawklike features and a pair of penetrating eyes. His mouth was thin and cruel.

"Yes, I have a mission for you, Jalor."

"Command me, Sire!"

"It concerns your kinsmen, the Shadow Wings. I have work for them to do. It concerns the Winged Raiders."

An expression of hatred flashed across the face of Jalor. "Chief White Storm is a strong warrior but a fool."

"He may be a fool, but his band is fierce. Can you engage the Shadow Wings in a battle against the Winged Raiders?"

Jalor hesitated. "It would be difficult, Sire. We would have to use trickery, but . . . but wait—I have a plan." He hesitated, then said, "The Dark Lord himself has commanded this?"

"Yes, and he also commands that you slay the Seven Sleepers. They have escaped time and time again. I cannot explain it. They are mere children, and they have eluded our most powerful attempts."

"They are the servants of Goél." Jalor nodded. "This time they will die. Let me explain my plan . . ."

10
Jalor Has a Plan

As the days passed and turned into weeks, the Sleepers began slowly to learn the difficult task of flying. All of them had difficulty, none more than Wash. The smallest of the Sleepers found himself having nightmares, for he had a deep fear of high places.

He said nothing to his friends, but Reb, who knew him better than any other, said one day, "It's gonna be all right, Wash. Goél doesn't want us to lose." He grinned, and the sun caught his sandy hair, and his blue eyes glowed. "Far as I know, Goél don't sponsor no losers."

Wash was dusting himself off. He had just taken a hard fall after coming in for a landing. "There's two things about this here flying I don't like," he said mournfully.

"What's that, Wash?"

"Going up—and coming down."

Reb laughed and slapped the smaller boy on the shoulder. "You're gonna love it before it's all done. Come on, let's go see how the girls are doing."

They made their way to another part of the plateau where they found Abbey and Sarah taking an advanced lesson from Lareen. The girls had been at it for more than three hours.

* * *

Lareen was giving them a pep talk. "It's a chance for us girls to catch up with the men," she told them. "I want to show everyone that girls can fly just as well as men and boys."

Abbey shook her head. "I don't think that'll ever work," she said. "Even if we did learn to do all this flying, we still wouldn't be as good with a bow, and we couldn't fight like the men."

But Lareen was adamant. "I'm going to prove you wrong, Abbey," she said. "Now this time, come on, and let's try a little formation flying."

"Look! Here comes Josh and Dave," Abbey said. "Maybe they want to go with us. And look! There's Wash and Reb."

"That's all of us except Jake," Sarah said. "No, here he comes." She motioned over to where Jake was approaching, and soon all seven of the Sleepers were gathered.

Lareen said, "This time we're going to try something fun. Have you ever seen a group of ducks when they fly in formation?"

"I have," Reb said. "Sometimes they make a V."

"That's right," Lareen said. "Now, I'll be the point of the V, and you line up on each side of me. Josh, you and Sarah and Reb get on one side. Dave, you get on the other side with Abigail, Jake, and Wash." She got them lined up and cried out, "Come on, let's go!"

Josh had learned to like flying, something he never thought he would. When he launched out, he watched the earth fall away. It was a wonderful feeling. The wind was whistling, blowing his hair back. He managed to spread his wings just right, and now all eight of them soared upward.

Lareen called out commands, and soon they had reached a current of air and formed a V. Far below Josh could see some of the tribe looking almost like ants. Far away he saw a river curling in long serpentine coils. There were spots of green in the various oases, and Josh thought, *If the people of the desert had a scout that could fly, they could always find water. Some of them have died of thirst just because they couldn't see it. Now that's an idea.*

Finally the lesson was over, and they came back to earth.

Afterward they went to have a meal, and Josh noticed that Swiftwind didn't get too far away from Lareen.

"You know what I think?" he said to Sarah, who was sitting beside him.

"Of course I know what you think," Sarah said calmly. She bit into a piece of freshly made bread, chewed on it thoughtfully, and said, "You're thinking that one of these days Swiftwind and Lareen are going to get married and live happily ever after."

Josh stared at her in astonishment. "How did you know I thought that?"

Sarah laughed. "Josh, your face is just like a book. You can't cover a thing that you feel. You've always been that way, even when we were growing up."

Josh stared at her solemnly. "I haven't thought about growing up in a long time." He ran his hand over his hair and looked at Sarah. "You're a lot different, Sarah."

"Different from what?"

"Different from the little girl who first came to live with us back on Oldworld. You're almost a woman now."

Sarah flushed and shot a quick glance at him. She was a graceful girl with bright, alert, brown eyes and very black hair that she had tied in a ponytail. She had changed, she knew, and so had Josh. He had always been very tall, but before he had been gangling and awkward. Now, at fifteen, he was filling out and with his auburn hair and almost electric blue eyes was turning into a fine-looking young man. She did not say so, however, but shrugged and said, "Well, we've come a long way since those days."

"What do you think is going to happen here?" Josh asked. He picked up a stick and drew a picture in the dirt.

"Flying is fun, but I don't see how we're making any headway."

"Why, Josh, that's not so!" Sarah said quickly. "We're not slaves anymore, and the chief is listening to us about Goél's ways more than I'd ever expected."

"Yes, but there's still a lot of people who don't believe in him." He had gotten a little discouraged. "I don't trust Darkwind. He smiles a lot, but have you ever noticed that his smiles don't go as far as his eyes?"

"Yes, I've noticed, and he's having more influence than he did when we first came."

"Come on, let's go talk to Jake. Maybe we can get Lareen convinced about Goél. Then she can convince her father."

The two went on their way—and were totally unaware that they had been watched by two figures.

* * *

Far above the plain where they had sat, Darkwind was talking with Jalor. Jalor turned now and said, "I have been commanded to destroy the Sleepers."

"Good!" Darkwind said. "I can see that they are going to be trouble." He moved restlessly and fingered the knife in his belt. It had a silver handle, and he was fond of pulling it out and testing its keen edge with his thumb. He did so now and said, "I will take care of them myself."

"No, it will not be that way," Jalor said. He was smaller than Darkwind, but there was a power in him that gave the younger man pause. "We need to do more than kill the Sleepers, although that is part of our task."

"Do you have a plan?"

"Yes, the Shadow Wings must take over this tribe. There's been too much time wasted trying to convert White Storm. He will never change."

"Then he must die too." Darkwind hesitated, then added, "That would put Swiftwind, his son, in as chief, and he's no better than his father."

Jalor turned his dark face toward the younger man. "If you will be obedient to me, *you* will be the chief of the Winged Raiders."

Instantly Darkwind nodded. He had a sinister face, and there was cruelty in his dark eyes. "I will do as you say. What is your plan?"

"Come, we will go on a little trip."

"Trip? Where will we go?"

"We will go to the Shadow Wings. Only a few of us have infiltrated White Storm's band, but we have done so without raising anyone's suspicion. The foolish White Storm thinks I am his loyal warrior! There is a way to accomplish our purpose. Come."

Jalor sprang into the air and was followed by Darkwind. The two soared high, headed toward the north where the Shadow Wings had their camp. As they went, both were thinking of what was to come.

Darkwind was thinking, *I will be chief. Then we shall see.*

But Jalor had only one thought: *Let Darkwind be chief if he pleases, but he will always bow his knee to the Dark Lord and to me.*

11
A New Kind of Hunt

Swiftwind found Lareen sitting beside Jake, the two of them with their backs to the wall of stone that rose high above them. They were staring out over the desert, and when Swiftwind lighted beside them he demanded, "What are you two doing here?"

"Oh, Garfield has been telling me how it was back in the world he came from. It's so exciting!"

Swiftwind had been rather jealous of Jake, although he knew it was foolish to feel such a thing for a mere slave. He was by far the most accomplished young man among the Raiders. He was able to fly faster, soar higher, and perform gymnastic feats beyond what any other young man could accomplish. Now, however, he said grumpily, "What did they have that we don't have here?"

"Oh, they had a lot of things," Lareen said. "Garfield was just telling me about something called a 'television.'"

"Television?" Swiftwind asked curiously. "What is a television?"

"It's a box, and you can see pictures on it."

"I don't care anything about drawing pictures. That's for girls."

"You'd like this," Lareen insisted. "You can see a picture that moves and talks."

"Moves and talks?" Swiftwind stared in disbelief at the two. He put his eyes on Jake saying, "You're making all that up. Pictures can't move and talk."

Jake shrugged. "Well, I know it's hard to believe for someone who hasn't seen it. But if I went back there and tried to tell my friends that there were people who could fly, they wouldn't believe that either."

"They don't fly in your world? What a dull place it must be!"

"Well," Jake said, "we flew, but not like you do. We didn't have wings."

"How could anybody fly without wings? Don't be a fool."

"I wish you could see a jet. Then you'd see something really fly."

"I don't know what a jet is, but if you like it so well there, I'm sorry you ever came here."

"Me too," Jake said angrily. He had a fiery temper and said defiantly, "That's the only thing you can do that we couldn't do—fly."

Swiftwind moved quicker than Jake could imagine. He grabbed the younger boy by the arms and dangled him over the cliff. "Let's see you fly—*without* wings!" he cried angrily.

"Let him go, Swiftwind!" Lareen cried out. She put her hands on Swiftwind's shoulders, and soon the three of them were engaged in a pulling contest.

In disgust, Swiftwind tossed Jake back on the ledge. "If you ask my opinion, they'd be better off hauling water and finding firewood. They'll never make warriors. They're too weak." He leaped into the air and, with a graceful turn, caught the breeze and sailed away. He was angry and for the rest of the day was snappy and irritable.

It was in this sort of mood that Jalor found him. The small, dark visitor came to where Swiftwind was sitting and saw at once the restlessness and anger in the eyes of the young man. He was clever, this Jalor, knowing men well and how to handle them, and his plan was continuing to evolve in his mind.

"Well, Swiftwind," he said, smiling, "how goes it with you?" He added slyly, "I see you've been talking to Lareen. She's a great admirer of the Sleepers, especially the red-headed one they call Garfield."

He knew the words would cause Swiftwind's temper to flare, which it did.

Swiftwind kicked at a stone and sent it flying. "They're worse than women," he said. "I don't know why my father doesn't put them back to work. They'll never be Raiders."

"I think you're right about that," Jalor agreed quickly. "Come, tell me what you've been doing."

The two walked along, and as the young man talked, the plan took final shape in the mind of the small, dark Jalor.

"It's a little dangerous to have visitors like that," he said, shrugging his shoulders. "They confuse things. Now, I've been watching how things are going, and it seems to me that there's a chance here for a young man with courage and daring to achieve something."

Quickly Swiftwind glanced at him. "What do you mean, Jalor?"

"Well, what's the one thing that would impress your father and the rest of the tribe?"

Instantly Swiftwind said, "To recover the lost crown of the Raiders. Ever since it was stolen by the Shadow Wings, it's been a shame on our people." He referred to a crown of gold that had been the greatest treasure of the Winged Raiders. It went far back in their history. It had been lost in a raid when the Shadow Wings had appeared suddenly. There had been a fierce battle. Many had been wounded and some killed, and the crown had been stolen.

"Exactly! I think if you could get that crown back there would be no question in Lareen's eyes when she looks at you. And your father would be pleased too."

93

Swiftwind was suddenly aflame with desire. "Do you know where the crown is, Jalor?"

"Well, I think I may say that I do. Not that I have anything to do with the Shadow Wings, but I met one of their elders once. He told me the whole story. Actually, it shouldn't be too hard to get it back. They're not expecting anyone to come. It's not in a well-guarded place."

"But, how could we get it? My father won't go to war. I've tried to talk him into that."

"I think I can be of some help to you. I have a map," Jalor said, lowering his voice to a whisper and looking around as though he expected the enemy to be behind him. "If you had just a little help, I think you might make it inside their lines."

"Would you go with me?"

"Why, of course," Jalor said.

"Good, I'll get some of my friends—"

"No, it would get back to your father. They are very loyal to him."

"But we have to have some help."

Jalor nodded. "This may sound surprising, but suppose we ask the Sleepers to go?"

"The *Sleepers?*" Swiftwind stared at him with astonishment. "What good are they? They're not warriors!"

"No, but they have some power. I don't understand it exactly, but the servants of Goél get things done when strong men fail. On a mission like this, I think they might be quite helpful."

Swiftwind looked doubtful, but he was burning with desire to go on with the feat. "All right. I'll talk to them. They've been saying they want to do something. This will give them a chance. But once we get the crown, I will tell my father to send them back to the chores of slaves."

"Good," Jalor said, "and I think you must move quickly. Let me know when the plan is ready."

"Yes, I'll talk to them today."

Swiftwind was as good as his word. He did not say a word to Lareen, for he knew she would be against the plan. Instead he went to Josh.

"Josh, you're the leader of your people. I have something to tell you." He set forth the plan, leaving out Jalor's part in it, and his eyes glowed with excitement. "We want the same thing," he said. "You want to convince my father and the tribe that Goél is strong, and I want to get the crown back. If we could do that, everyone would admit that Goél is worthy."

Josh was wary. "Well, it sounds good," he admitted reluctantly. "We're not getting very far where we are, but you understand we're not Raiders. That is, we're not strong warriors."

"I know that, but if Goél has any power, it's with you. *I'm* going," he said defiantly, "even if I have to go alone."

"Wait!" Josh said. He stood hesitantly, then added, "We'll have a meeting. I can't decide this by myself."

"Good, but it must be fast. There's no time to waste."

Josh left Swiftwind and called the group together. He led them to an open spot in the desert where no one could possibly overhear, and he set Swiftwind's proposition before them. He ended his story by saying slowly, "I just don't know whether it's the right thing to do or not. It sounds good, but if something goes wrong, it could be bad."

A debate started at once. Reb Jackson, as Josh had guessed, was all in favor of going, but Abigail and Sarah were not so sure.

Sarah said slowly, "I wish Goél were here to tell us what to do. It's awful just having to guess like this. Maybe we'd better wait. He may come at any time."

k his head, saying loudly, "Why, shoot, if
d, we'll never get anything done. This is our
e better take it."

wly nodded his head. "I think I agree with
like just the thing to win the confidence of

The debate went on for some time. For some rea-
son, the plan did not sit well with Jake. He said, "I know
we need to do something, but I'm not sure this is it.
Swiftwind is too impulsive. We don't know anything about
those Shadow Wings. And neither does he, except that he
hates them."

"He really does," Sarah said, "and that's bad. We've
got to convince him and these other people somehow that
hatred won't do."

"Well, we've got our hands full, but I think I'll vote
for going," Wash said.

"Well, then," Josh spoke up, "I guess that's the ma-
jority. I'll go tell Swiftwind, and I guess we'd better get
ready to go. He's really anxious."

* * *

The sky was still dark, although dawn was beginning
to glimmer in the east as the Sleepers glided through the
cool air. They were led by Swiftwind and Jalor, who had
brought them in a roundabout way to the camp of the
Shadow Wings.

"There is the camp below," Jalor cried out. He gestured toward the earth and even in the dim murkiness
Josh could see small glowing fires.

"Let's go!" Swiftwind cried out.

Jalor said quickly, "We've gone over the plan. I'll stay
up here as a sentinel. When you get the crown, fly back. If
anyone follows, I'll fight a rearguard action myself."

96

14
Jake Has a Plan

Jake did not disturb the others, but for the rest of the long night he was awake. Always before it had been Josh or Sarah or Dave—one of the others—who had received information from Goél. He remembered suddenly how at their first encounter with the Sanhedrin and the Dark Lord they had been imprisoned. The dungeon had been as dark as this one, and their outlook just as gloomy. It had been Sarah who had announced suddenly that Goél had come to her, and Jake had been one of those, he remembered, who had said, "We didn't see him. You must have been dreaming."

Now, as Jake looked over the sleeping forms, he wondered if they would have the same reaction when he told them. *Doesn't make any difference, he thought, I've got to do what Goél commands.* He felt inadequate and wondered why it hadn't been Dave or Josh or Reb who had been entrusted with this thing. But Jake was a stubborn young man and now knew that the plan Goél had revealed to him he would have to share with the others. He hated to be teased or doubted, and he knew that was exactly what he faced.

Finally Dave began to stir, then sat up groaning. In doing so, he bumped against Reb, who moaned and said, "Let me alone!" Then he, too, came awake. Their stirrings roused the others, and Jake watched as one by one they came out of their sleep and began to look around.

Josh blinked and licked his lips. Looking around the cell, he said, "Well, seems like the story of our life, doesn't it? Always in a prison of some kind or other."

113

Reb stretched hugely, yawned, and said, "Sure does, and this time it might not work out as well as it has before." He looked toward the door as if expecting the executioner to come walking in, then turned to look at Jake, who was standing off to one side, his back to the cold wall. "What's wrong with you, Jake?" he asked.

Jake cleared his throat and said, "Well, I think we're all right—in a way."

"All right!" Wash yelped. "Here we are in a dungeon, going to be executed, and you say we're all right! I don't think your elevator's going all the way up, Jake."

Jake had to smile at the small black boy. He said quickly, "I had a visit from Goél."

Instantly every one of the other Sleepers turned and stared at him. It was Reb who demanded, "Well, what did he say, Jake?"

Jake was warmly grateful to Reb for not questioning his statement, and he saw the same assurance in the others' eyes. *At least we've learned something,* he thought. *To trust each other.* Aloud he said, "He told me that it was the right thing to do, to come here, and I guess I've got to apologize to you, Josh, and the rest of you for being such a pain in the neck."

"Did he say why he never *told* us to come?" Dave demanded.

"Yes, he did," Jake said. "He said that we had to learn to walk sometimes without direct orders. Somehow that seemed important to him. He called it a walk of faith." He shrugged his shoulders, adding, "I don't like it, and I know you don't either, but that's what he said."

Josh came over to stand next to Jake. Excitement was in his face, and he said, "What else did he say, Jake?"

"He said a lot, but the first thing is that we've got to get an audience with the chief before we get killed."

"Better before than after, I always say." Reb grunted. "Did he say how to do it?"

"No, but I guess we just ask for it."

As it turned out, they did not find it difficult. Sure Flight and his daughter, Lareen, came into their cell not thirty minutes later. Lareen ran at once to Jake and said, "Garfield, are you all right?"

"I am right now," Jake said, "but things don't look too promising."

Lareen looked at her father and said, "Can't we do something?"

Sure Flight said, "You know what he's like. When the chief gets stubborn, I don't think anything could change his mind."

Jake said, "I believe I can help if I can just talk to him. Won't you please try to get me an audience?"

Sure Flight looked at him carefully. "I will try," he said.

He turned and left the cell, and as soon as he was gone Lareen said, "I know you're worried about Sarah. I am too. And Swiftwind. They're in the hands of terrible people."

There was a silence that ran around the room, and then Josh said, "We've been in some tight spots, Lareen, and always before Goél has gotten us out of them."

Lareen did not look convinced. "I'm not sure about that," she said, "but I'm worried sick about Swiftwind."

At once Abigail went over and put her arm around the girl. "I won't tell you not to worry," she said quietly, "but I will tell you that we've seen Goél do great and mighty things."

Lareen stared at her and then shook her head.

For a while the group talked quietly among themselves, everyone listening for a footfall out in the corridor.

115

Finally the lock on the door made a loud click, and the door opened.

Sure Flight came in, saying, "Quickly, you have an audience with the chief." He looked at Jake. "You will have to speak quickly. He is very hard."

The guards were waiting outside and accompanied the Sleepers all the way to the chambers of Chief White Storm. Darkwind was there, as was Jalor, and Jake wished they weren't.

"You have something to say to me?" White Storm said in a forbidding voice. His face was stern, and his eyes were cold—or perhaps one might say hot—with anger. He loved this son of his and blamed the Sleepers for his capture.

Jake at once knew that it was up to him. He stepped forward and said, "Chief White Storm, I understand your grief over your son. We know grief too, for our friend Sarah is also a captive."

"She will not be killed. She will only be made a slave," White Storm said harshly.

Jake wanted to argue that being a slave of the Shadow Wings was not much different from being dead. However, he said only, "I will not quarrel with that." He knew he had to speak quickly and said at once, "I have a plan to get your son and Sarah back."

"A plan? What is it?"

Jake glanced quickly at Jalor and Darkwind and said, "I am under command of Goél. I can speak only to you, Chief White Storm."

At once Jalor said, "He's a liar, like all the rest."

Darkwind nodded. "He's only trying to get out of being executed. You can't blame him for that, but you can't believe anything he says."

Lareen said quickly, "Chief White Storm, you know how I feel about Swiftwind, and I know how you feel about your son. Please, this may be our only chance. We have gotten to know Garfield very well. He is not a liar. Please listen to him."

Silence fell around the chamber. It seemed to be thick, and the Sleepers waited, seeing their lives hanging in the balance. Finally White Storm nodded slowly. "I will hear what you have to say. The rest of you, leave us."

Jalor began to protest, echoed by Darkwind, but one look from White Storm quieted them. They left with the others, their brows dark with anger.

As soon as they were out of the chamber, Jake said, "First, I thank you, Chief, for listening to me. I know that you are hurt and grieving over your son. I only ask you to believe that I, too, am grieved. All of us are."

"What is this plan you have?" White Storm demanded harshly.

"From what I understand, you are planning to go with your warriors and attack the Shadow Wings."

"There is nothing else I can do."

"But it looks pretty hopeless, doesn't it?" Jake asked. "They'll be waiting for you."

"Yes, they will, but what can a man do?" White Storm hesitated and said, "He is my only son, the hope of all our people."

Jake said, "Let me tell you just a little about our adventures. I know time is short, but you need to know more about Goél."

Again White Storm hesitated, then he nodded. "Tell me," he said quietly.

For the next thirty minutes, Jake spoke as rapidly as he could. He was actually a good speaker and a fine story-teller. He traced the adventures of the Seven Sleepers since they had come out of their time capsules. He told of how they had been in hopeless situations, sentenced to death, and trapped. He painted the grim problems they

117

had encountered, the dangers, the weariness. And then he told how in each case Goél had given them escape. Then he said, his eyes bright, "Chief White Storm, Goél came to me last night."

"Impossible! He could not get inside the jail."

Jake shrugged. "I don't know how he does it. Maybe it was in a dream. That's the way he does sometimes, but he's always there, and he told me how we could get your son and Sarah free and also how you could conquer the Shadow Wings."

Chief White Storm once again fell silent. His dark eyes were thoughtful, and finally he leaned forward and said, "Very well. There is no hope in a direct attack. Tell me what Goél commands."

Jake felt a thrill of victory as the chief said this. He knew that it was a hard thing for this man to say, a man who was accustomed to having his own way. He was a stern, hard man, but deep down Jake felt he could become a much better man.

"Here is what Goél said." Then he repeated exactly what Goél had told him. When he had finished, he nodded. "That is what he said, Chief. Now you must decide what you will do."

White Storm dropped his head. He seemed to be studying the floor as if there were some intricate pattern there. The silence ran on. Jake dared not say a word.

Finally White Storm lifted his head, and there was a flicker of hope in his dark eyes. "We will try the way of Goél," he said heavily, then rose to his feet. "Come, we have much to do!"

15

The Rescue

Chief Ali had arisen early. He had been despondent, for he could not help but think of how his people had been made captives. Each year more of them were taken by the Winged Raiders. Only two nights before, the Shadow Wings had taken three more of his most promising people and slain two of his best warriors.

He sipped slowly at a cup of water, thinking of how little hope there was ahead for his people. Abdul came to sit beside him, and for a time the two talked of the problems that had beset the tribe.

"I had hoped that the Sleepers, as they are called, might have helped us," Chief Ali said.

Ali looked downcast. "I, too, had confidence in them, but they are beyond hope now. They've either fallen to the Shadow Wings or to the Winged Raiders of Chief White Storm. In any case, no one escapes either of them." The two men sat silently, and finally Ali rose slowly. "We will have to take our bands out, away from our homes," he said finally.

"We cannot leave our homeland, Chief Ali," Abdul protested.

Pain was in the chief's eyes. He stood there, a tall figure, his skin burned to the color of old copper and set off by his white hair. "We have no other choice. We must leave here, or we will all be the slaves of the Winged Raiders."

All that day, Chief Ali wandered, looking up often at the sky as had become his custom. The Raiders never

119

made a direct attack on the camp, for there were armed men there ready to protect the Desert People. It was the wandering bands and the isolated families that got too far away whom they made their captives. He finally turned wearily and headed back toward the camp. Even as he turned, something caught his eye—something overhead.

Instantly he shaded his eyes with his hand. It might be only a bird, but there was always the chance it was one of the Raiders.

As soon as he looked, he murmured, "It is not a bird."

Almost he lifted his voice to cry aloud, but he did not. "There is only one of them," he said. He quickly removed his sword from his sash and stood waiting. He could not believe that a Raider would come alone. Yet still, as he watched, he saw surely it was a flying man, not a bird.

Closer and closer the form came. At first, only a dot, then growing larger. Ali realized that he had been seen. He planted his feet and gritted his teeth. "Come to me," he whispered, "I will feed your body to the jackals of the desert!"

The wind whistled, drowning out his words. He kept his eyes fixed steadily on the Winged Raider and saw that he was dropping straight toward him. Planting his feet, he said, "Now, we shall see."

Steadily the Raider dropped. Then the huge wings suddenly spread, and Ali held his sword in the guard position.

"Chief Ali, it's me, Jake Garfield."

Chief Ali Shareef had never been so shocked. He knew, of course, that the Winged Raiders wore wings that were made, not grown, but still . . .

"Is it you, my son?" he gasped and ran forward to meet Jake. He stared at the young man stopping in front of him and shook his head in wonder. "How is it that you fly? Are you now one of the Winged Raiders?"

"No, never that," Jake said quickly. His eyes were tired, for he had had a long flight. He had been afraid that he would lose his way over the trackless desert and indeed he had, but he had received good instructions from White Storm and now, though he was tired, he said, "I bring you good news," he said. "Goél is with us."

Chief Ali stared at the young man. He could not help examining the wings curiously and asking, "How did you learn all of this? How is it you are not a slave?"

"There's no time to explain right now," Jake said wearily. He lifted his shoulders, and his body almost ached with the effort he had made. Flying was harder work than it looked. It took constant adjustments to change the flight to meet the different changes of the wind. He said quickly, "We must go at once to the Citadel, you and all your armed men."

Chief Ali stared. "What is this?" he asked quietly. "Tell me what has happened." He stood listening as Jake recounted his adventures, and his eyes grew wide with wonder. Finally he interrupted to ask, "What does it all mean, your coming here? If the others have wings, why could they not escape too?"

"Because there's a war between the Shadow Wings and the Winged Raiders."

"They're all the same to me," Chief Ali snapped. "Those who come out of the sky never bring anything but evil to my people."

Jake had thought about this on his long journey. He had also planned a speech. "There is a difference, Chief," he said quickly. "The Shadow Wings are the servants of the Dark Lord, whereas White Storm and his band are not. What we must do is to assist the Winged Raiders to defeat the Shadow Wings. Then we can arrange a peace between your people and the people of Chief White Storm."

Chief Ali listened as Jake outlined the plan. He had difficulty accepting what the young man told him, but Jake became very persuasive. At last he said, "You'll find Chief White Storm a man of honor even as you yourself are. If you could only sit down and talk to him, the two of you would learn to respect one another."

"I can hardly believe that," Chief Ali said. "Nevertheless, if there is any hope, I am willing to try. Tell me more of this plan you have come with." He continued to listen and, when he had heard it all, he took a deep breath and stood impassively, his eyes fixed on the face of the young man.

Jake could not read beyond the features of the chief. He thought at first Ali meant to refuse, but then the chief nodded, saying, "We will try it." He hesitated, then said, "We will see if Goél is with you or not, my young friend."

* * *

All around the camp there were stirrings as the Winged Raiders prepared themselves for the battle to come. Ever since Jake had come back and held a secret conference with Chief White Storm, all knew that great things were underfoot. The chief at once gave the order that all warriors were to be prepared, but he gave no details.

Jalor stood watching as the warriors worked on their arrows, sharpened their swords and daggers, and balanced their spears carefully to be sure they were true. Sure Flight, the chief's second-in-command, would lead the attack. He came now to stand before Jalor. His dark reddish hair gleamed in the early morning sunlight, and he demanded, "Well, Jalor, will you fight with us?"

Instantly Jalor nodded. "Yes, I will be honored to be among the ranks of the valorous Raiders." He smiled, but as soon as Sure Flight turned and left, he also moved away.

He was walking along the edge of the huge cliff staring out in the direction of Shadow Wing territory when he heard footsteps. Turning, he saw Darkwind approaching. "Were you able to discover the plan?"

"No, they will tell me nothing," Jalor snapped. "That is your responsibility; you are one of them. You should be able to uncover the strategy."

A snarl curled Darkwind's lips upward. "I have tried, but the chief will say nothing, nor will Sure Flight. We are told simply that we will leave the Citadel, and tonight we will be told the final battle plan."

"White Storm is a wise battle leader," Jalor said slowly. "No chance of a leak that way." He fingered his dagger thoughtfully, murmuring, "We will have to make our plans as we go. As soon as we find out the plan, I will slip away and alert our friends on the other side."

The two men parted then, and Darkwind went at once to his unit. Jalor wandered among the warriors, studying their faces and wishing he knew what was in the mind of Chief White Storm.

Jake looked around the circle of his friends and said, "Well, this is it—our last chance. If we fail, I think we'll all be executed. Chief White Storm has given us this one chance, but he's still not totally convinced. Only a victory will do that."

Josh looked over his shoulder. They had been released from their confinement and were to join in the attack, for Sure Flight believed in them, and the Winged Raiders needed every warrior they could get. "What is the plan, Jake?" he asked. "All the warriors are a little confused. I don't think it's usual to go to a battle without knowing how they're going to fight."

"That was my idea," Jake said, then grinned. "Well, not really. It was Goél's idea. He said to let no one know the battle strategy until just before the attack. But I can tell you." Even though the nearest Raider was fifty feet away, he lowered his voice and whispered, "You see, the Shadow Wings have never been attacked except from the air. In the last war with the Winged Raiders, that was what it amounted to. The Shadow Wings live like the Raiders, on a high peak. It takes a great deal of skill just to get up there. But there is a way."

Reb said, "I know, just like Old Stonewall Jackson. He was always sneaking around and coming at the enemy from behind. He done that at Chancellorsville."

"You're right, Reb," Jake nodded. "What we will do is make what we call a feint. The Shadow Wings will be looking up at the sky, expecting the enemy to come from there. They won't be looking behind them at the passes. They'll have every warrior they've got right on the front line. So we'll draw them off, draw them away from safety, and as soon as they leave, Chief Ali and his men will come up the slope and take the ground."

Dave exclaimed, "And they won't have any home base to go back to!"

Abigail said, "It was like that in one of the wars in Oldworld when they had aircraft carriers. Once a group of pilots left the deck they had no place to go. If the carrier was sunk, they were lost."

"That's it. Pretty simple." Jake nodded. "The timing is the tough thing. Chief Ali can't move up the slope until we draw the Shadow Wings into battle, and we can't move the Winged Raiders into battle until Chief Ali is ready."

"Sounds like a hard thing to me," Wash said. Then his white teeth flashed. "But I guess you can handle it, Jake."

Jake flushed. "We all know better than that," he said, "but it's our one chance. All of us are going," he said. "Not that some of us are any good as warriors, but at least we add numbers, and that's what we've got to do—impress the Shadow Wings with our force."

"Well," Josh scratched his head thoroughly, worry in his eyes, "I'll do anything to get Sarah back. We all will. Let's agree here that once the battle starts, our job is to find Sarah and Swiftwind. Goél won't let us down. We'll find them."

* * *

An early dawn attack was the plan. The force had left the Citadel after dark so that no spies from the Shadow Wings could see them crossing the skies. Sure Flight led them in a roundabout direction, and they spent the night on a peak not five miles away from the mountain where the Shadow Wings had their camp.

Now all the warriors were gathered around, listening as Sure Flight gave them their instructions. The wind was cool, and the Sleepers stood huddled in a bunch, listening carefully.

"We will attack at dawn," Sure Flight said. "We must allow ourselves to be seen. That way we can draw the enemy's attention to ourselves."

Instantly Darkwind cried out, "Why should we allow ourselves to be seen? I say always we want to surprise the enemy." His eyes met those of Jalor across the way, who nodded shortly. "I say the battle plan is bad."

Sure Flight raised his voice. "You're not the battle chief of the Raiders, Darkwind. Not yet. There is more to this battle plan than you know, and now the time has come to reveal it. We have allies in this battle."

A murmur went around the warriors, and Jalor asked the question they all had. "And who are these allies, sir?"

Sure Flight kept his eyes fixed on Jalor and said evenly, "The Desert People—they will fight with us against the Shadow Wings."

"They are our *enemies*," Darkwind cried in astonishment.

"Not any longer," Sure Flight said firmly. "It is our only hope. We will draw the Shadow Wings into the air. Chief Ali and his troops are waiting at the foot of the mountain, well hidden. When the Shadow Wings take to the air to pursue us, the Desert People will charge up the slope and take the base. And then there will be no place for the Shadow Wings to return to. They will be trapped."

Sure Flight gave firm instructions. "You will come in squadrons. I will lead the first. We have two purposes: one is to defeat the Shadow Wings, but more important, we must rescue the son of Chief White Storm. We must have Swiftwind and the Sleeper Sarah."

Jalor said smoothly, "I believe I can help with that. I know something about these people. I believe I could find the captives if you would permit me to pursue it."

Sure Flight hesitated. He knew that Jalor had some knowledge of the Shadow Wings. This had been the flaw in the plan. He and White Storm and Jake had all considered the possibility that the Shadow Wings would kill the captives before allowing them to be retaken. After a moment's hesitation, he nodded. "Very well. You will take the Sleepers and lead them to the prison and set the captives free."

Jake leaned over and whispered to Josh. "I don't like that much. I'd rather we just hunted and found them ourselves. I don't trust that guy." But there was no time, for Sure Flight was calling out for an instant departure.

"The sun will be up. See, already it turns the eastern skies red." He lifted his fist and shouted, "We will win this battle! The Winged Raiders will defeat their enemies! Come, by squadrons—"

None of the Sleepers ever forgot that flight! The sky seemed filled with winged men led by Sure Flight and the other squadron commanders. Jake and the other Sleepers flew in the last wave, and he could see as they looked down that they had been noticed.

"Look, they're coming up! They must have been ready!" Jake called to Lareen, who flew close to his side. She had elected to come with the Sleepers despite her father's objections.

"Yes." Lareen clasped a bow in her hand and notched an arrow. She called out, "We will stay as far from the fighting as we can."

Jalor, who was close by, said, "As soon as the fighting starts, we will slip away and come in from the easterly direction."

The battle began at once. It reminded Reb of movies that he had seen of air war. The Shadow Wings were indeed as black as night. They came furiously, and soon the air was filled with arrows and with a clash of sword on sword. Warriors grappled, fighting fiercely with daggers. Jake saw two of them drop toward the ground fighting until one of them slipped away limply to fall to the earth. There were screams and cries of battle and such confusion that the Sleepers could make nothing of it.

At that moment Jalor said, "Come, this way!" He soared off to the right, and the Sleepers followed him. Soon they were out of range of the battle sounds, and Jalor made a swooping turn. "This way!" he cried.

The little group landed on an open space in a wooded plateau. "The prison is that way," Jalor said. He looked at Jake. "Garfield, you lead the force. I will cover the rear. That is where the trouble will come from."

Jake was glad to be rid of Jalor. "Where is it?" he said. They all listened as Jalor gave the simple instructions, then turned and ran across the rock. Jake's heart was beating like a trip-hammer, and he looked across to see that Wash was panting hard too. "Don't fall behind, Wash," he said. "We've got to stick together."

Reb and Dave led the attack. They found the entrance to the cave guarded by only two warriors. The Shadow Wing guards let out a cry, but both young men had brought their bows. They loosed an arrow apiece, and both guards went down.

"Come on!" Reb yelled and uttered a wild, screeching cry. "Let's get them Yankees!"

"They're not Yankees," Dave said. "They're Shadow Wings."

"Oh, yeah, I forgot."

Then they were inside the cave. It was dark, but they made their way to a large steel door. Reb had brought the key from the belt of one of the guards and unlocked the door.

At once Sarah burst out. She threw herself at Josh, who grabbed her to keep her from falling.

"Sarah," he said, "are you all right?"

"Yes, I'm so glad you've come. I knew you would."

"Come on. We've got to get out of here. Are you all right, Swiftwind?"

Swiftwind stared at Jake, his face wearing an odd expression. He was silent for a moment, then nodded. "I see now that the servants of Goél are faithful, and so it must be that I will serve Goél. I and all my people when I am chief."

"No one is serving Goél."

They all whirled to see Jalor standing there, and behind him a group of Shadow Wings all carrying swords.

Jalor grinned triumphantly. "The plan has failed," he announced. "Now all of you are my prisoners."

What happened at that moment triggered what would later be called the Battle of the Cave.

The smile on the face of Jalor infuriated Lareen. "You traitor!" she cried and threw herself forward, pulling the short sword out of her belt.

Jalor, caught off guard by the audacious young woman, managed to draw his own sword, but her blade caught it and sent it spinning. At the same time, Jake yelled, "Sleepers, fight for the honor of Goél!"

Fortunately Jalor had brought only four armed men. They attacked, but two of them died at once as Reb and Dave loosed their arrows. The other two went down as Wash, Jake, Abbey, Josh, and Sarah threw themselves forward. Ordinarily it would not have been possible for young people to overcome these warriors, but the fury of their attack overwhelmed the Shadow Wings.

Lareen held the point of her blade to the throat of Jalor who began crying, "Don't kill me! Don't kill me!"

"You're a traitor," she said. "We will let the chief decide." Then she turned to Swiftwind, who had joined in the attack and said, "Now we will see what Goél can do for our people. Come. Let us see how the battle goes!"

16

A Time of Peace

The victory banquet was a tremendous success!

Chief White Storm sat beside Chief Ali Shareef, and after a sumptuous feast Chief White Storm stood and lifted his silver goblet. "May I have your attention!" He waited until those who packed the banquet hall, which was carved out of stone in a magnificent cave, paused to listen. The chief raised his goblet again, saying, "I give you our gallant allies, Chief Ali Shareef and the Desert People." He turned to face the chief, a smile on his face. "Our history will record the beginning of a time of peace between the Winged Raiders and the People of the Desert."

At once Chief Ali Shareef arose and lifted his own goblet. "And I propose a toast to Chief White Storm, a gallant warrior, and to his gallant people. May our two peoples live together in peace and harmony."

A cry ran around the hall, and Jake leaned back and basked in the admiration of the elders of both tribes. After the battle, which had been won by the arrival of the warriors of Chief Ali's band, the negotiations between the two chiefs had been brief and very cordial. The animosity that had existed between the two peoples seemed to go up in smoke.

Jake leaned over and whispered to Josh, "I guess they'll be able to get along now, but they'll always have lots of arguments about how to do it, I suppose. Any big group's like that."

"The big thing is," Josh said, a warm smile on his face, "they've found how to work together. The Desert

People can supply the Winged Raiders with things they need, and the Winged Raiders will agree to live at peace with them."

Lareen, sitting across the table with Swiftwind, looked at them quickly.

Swiftwind said, "It'll mean no more slavery. That's part of the agreement my father made with Chief Ali, and a good thing too."

"Yes, the slaves were so happy to be going back to their people!" Sarah exclaimed. She glanced over at Jake and said, "Well, Jake, you're the big hero. I expect they'll give you a medal or something."

Jake said slowly and thoughtfully, "I don't need a medal, but I sure learned a lot from this. Mostly about how to have faith in Goél."

"It did look pretty dark, didn't it?" Wash said. "I felt like I was walking through a graveyard at midnight, expecting somebody to get me at any minute. But it's all right now."

The banquet went on for some time, and at the end, when Josh as leader of the Seven Sleepers was asked to address the chiefs of both tribes, he rose and said, "I will not make a long speech, but I will say how happy I am to see the Winged Raiders and the Desert People come together." He hesitated, then said, "I have one request."

"Nothing you ask will be refused," Chief White Storm said instantly.

"It is a hard thing," Josh warned.

Chief White Storm said, "You will see that the Winged Raiders of the Desert know how to keep their word. What is your command?"

"Not a command, but a request," Josh said quietly. Every face was turned toward him, and absolute silence reigned. "I ask that you show mercy to the Shadow Wings," he said quietly. The silence grew even more profound, and then a murmur ran across the hall.

"The Shadow Wings!" White Storm was shocked. "But they are our enemies!"

"So were the Desert People, but now you are brothers," Josh said.

He began to speak of love and of how love could transform. His words were simple, but both chiefs and all their men appeared to be caught up in them.

"I never knew you could be so eloquent," Sarah said after the banquet was over. "I could tell that Chief White Storm was impressed."

The following day the two of them were walking along the edge of the Citadel, looking down on the desert far away. The Sleepers had come together for one final flight. As the others were putting on their wings, Josh said, "I think it's what Goél sent us here for—to bring the message of love to all of these people. Now, let's have one more flight."

Thirty minutes later, the Sleepers were soaring over the Citadel. They caught an updraft and rose in the air like birds. They turned and wheeled and glided, and, when they finally came to earth again, Josh said, "I'm going to miss all of this. We all will." He looked up and said, "Look! I believe the whole tribe's come to tell us good-bye."

"Well, I'm glad we don't have to ride a camel all the way back. At least we get one last long flight," Jake said.

They advanced to where the tribe was waiting with White Storm and Sure Flight. Beside them were Swiftwind and Lareen. Off to one side, Darkwind with a shamed look on his face watched but said nothing.

Jake had to feel sorry for him and muttered, "I'm trying to feel some of this love Goél is talking about, but it's hard to do with a cat like that!"

White Storm said, "I wish you would change your mind and remain with us," he said. "We would be proud to have you as members of the Winged Raiders."

Speaking for the group, Josh said, "It is an honor that we must refuse, O Chief. We must be obedient to Goél."

Lareen said, "But you will come back, won't you, Garfield?"

Jake said, "I sure hope so."

Chief White Storm said, "We will send an honor guard with you. They will see you safely to your homes and bring your wings back to the Citadel. They will be waiting for you when you come back."

It was a hard moment for Jake, for he had learned to love the people here. And as he sprang into the air he heard Lareen calling out, "Come back, Garfield! We'll be waiting for you!"

It was a long flight, but finally the honor guard, led by Sure Flight, set them down close to their village where they had first conceived the idea of visiting the Citadel. Sadly they removed their wings, gave them to the attendants, and Sure Flight bade them good-bye.

"Come back," he said. "We will be your people."

The Sleepers watched as the Winged Raiders rose and became mere dots and then disappeared.

"Well, back to the old drawing board." Jake sighed. "It seems like we do this over and over again, just one task after another."

Abigail slipped her arm through his. "Come on, Jake. You can tell me again what a big hero you are." The others laughed, but Abigail squeezed him. "I really mean that, Jake. You came out better than any of us this time. I believe you've taught us how to have more faith."

"Well, I was the one who didn't want to go," Jake protested, "but I'll be more ready next time, you can bet."

The Sleepers trudged back down the road. It was growing dark, and, as usual, Sarah fell into step with Josh. "It was hard, but I wouldn't trade it for anything," Sarah said.

To her surprise, Josh reached down and took her hand. That was an unusual thing for him to do, and she looked at him with surprise.

Josh was aware of her eyes and said, "I guess a fellow can hold hands with his girl if he wants to, can't he?"

It was something that Sarah had wanted to hear him say for a long time. She became choked up and was unable to speak. His hand was warm and strong and made her feel secure.

Finally he said, "You *are* my girl, aren't you, Sarah?"

Sarah gave him a warm smile. "Whose other girl would I be?" she whispered. "Come on, Josh," she cried, "let's go see what Goél has in store for us next."

Get swept away in the many Gilbert Morris Adventures available from Moody Press:

"Too Smart" Jones

4025-8 Pool Part Thief
4026-6 Buried Jewels
4027-4 Disappearing Dogs
4028-2 Dangerous Woman
4029-0 Stranger in the Cave
4030-4 Cat's Secret
4031-2 Stolen Bicycle
4032-0 Wilderness Mystery

Come along for the adventures and mysteries Juliet "Too Smart" Jones always manages to find. She and her other homeschool friends solve these great adventures and learn biblical truths along the way. Ages 9-14

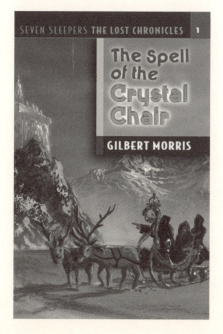

Seven Sleepers - The Lost Chronicles

3667-6 The Spell of the Crystal Chair
3668-4 The Savage Game of Lord Zarak
3669-2 The Strange Creatures of Dr. Korbo
3670-6 City of the Cyborgs

More exciting adventures from the Seven Sleepers. As these exciting young people attempt to faithfully follow Goel, they learn important moral and spiritual lessons. Come along with them as they encounter danger, intrigue, and mystery. Ages 10-14

Dixie Morris Animal Adventures

3363-4 Dixie and Jumbo
3364-2 Dixie and Stripes
3365-0 Dixie and Dolly
3366-9 Dixie and Sandy
3367-7 Dixie and Ivan
3368-5 Dixie and Bandit
3369-3 Dixie and Champ
3370-7 Dixie and Perry
3371-5 Dixie and Blizzard
3382-3 Dixie and Flash

Follow the exciting adventures of this animal lover as she learns more of God and His character through her many adventures underneath the Big Top. Ages 9-14

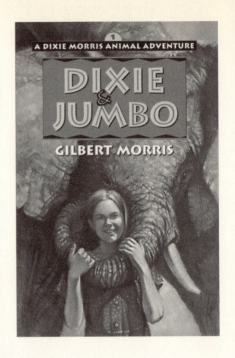

The Daystar Voyages

4102-X Secret of the Planet Makon
4106-8 Wizards of the Galaxy
4107-6 Escape From the Red Comet
4108-4 Dark Spell Over Morlandria
4109-2 Revenge of the Space Pirates
4110-6 Invasion of the Killer Locusts
4111-4 Dangers of the Rainbow Nebula
4112-2 The Frozen Space Pilot

Join the crew of the Daystar as they traverse the wide expanse of space. Adventure and danger abound, but they learn time and again that God is truly the Master of the Universe. Ages 10-14

Seven Sleepers Series

3681-1 Flight of the Eagles
3682-X The Gates of Neptune
3683-3 The Swords of Camelot
3684-6 The Caves That Time Forgot
3685-4 Winged Riders of the Desert
3686-2 Empress of the Underworld
3687-0 Voyage of the Dolphin
3691-9 Attack of the Amazons
3692-7 Escape with the Dream Maker
3693-5 The Final Kingdom

Go with Josh and his friends as they are sent by Goel, their spiritual leader, on dangerous and challenging voyages to conquer the forces of darkness in the new world. Ages 10-14

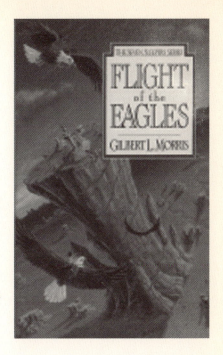

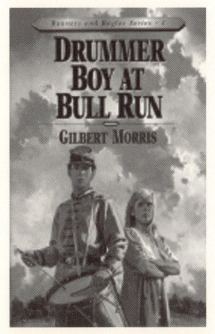

Bonnets and Bugles Series

0911-3 Drummer Boy at Bull Run
0912-1 Yankee Bells in Dixie
0913-X The Secret of Richmond Manor
0914-8 The Soldier Boy's Discovery
0915-6 Blockade Runner
0916-4 The Gallant Boys of Gettysburg
0917-2 The Battle of Lookout Mountain
0918-0 Encounter at Cold Harbor
0919-9 Fire Over Atlanta
0920-2 Bring the Boys Home

Follow good friends Leah Carter and Jeff Majors as they experience danger, intrigue, compassion, and love in these civil war adventures. Ages 10-14

Moody Press, a ministry of the Moody Bible Institute,
is designed for education, evangelization, and edification.
If we may assist you in knowing more about Christ
and the Christian life, please write us without obligation:
Moody Press, c/o MLM, Chicago, Illinois 60610.